For all those who choose to escape in books and fall for the villains. This is for you...

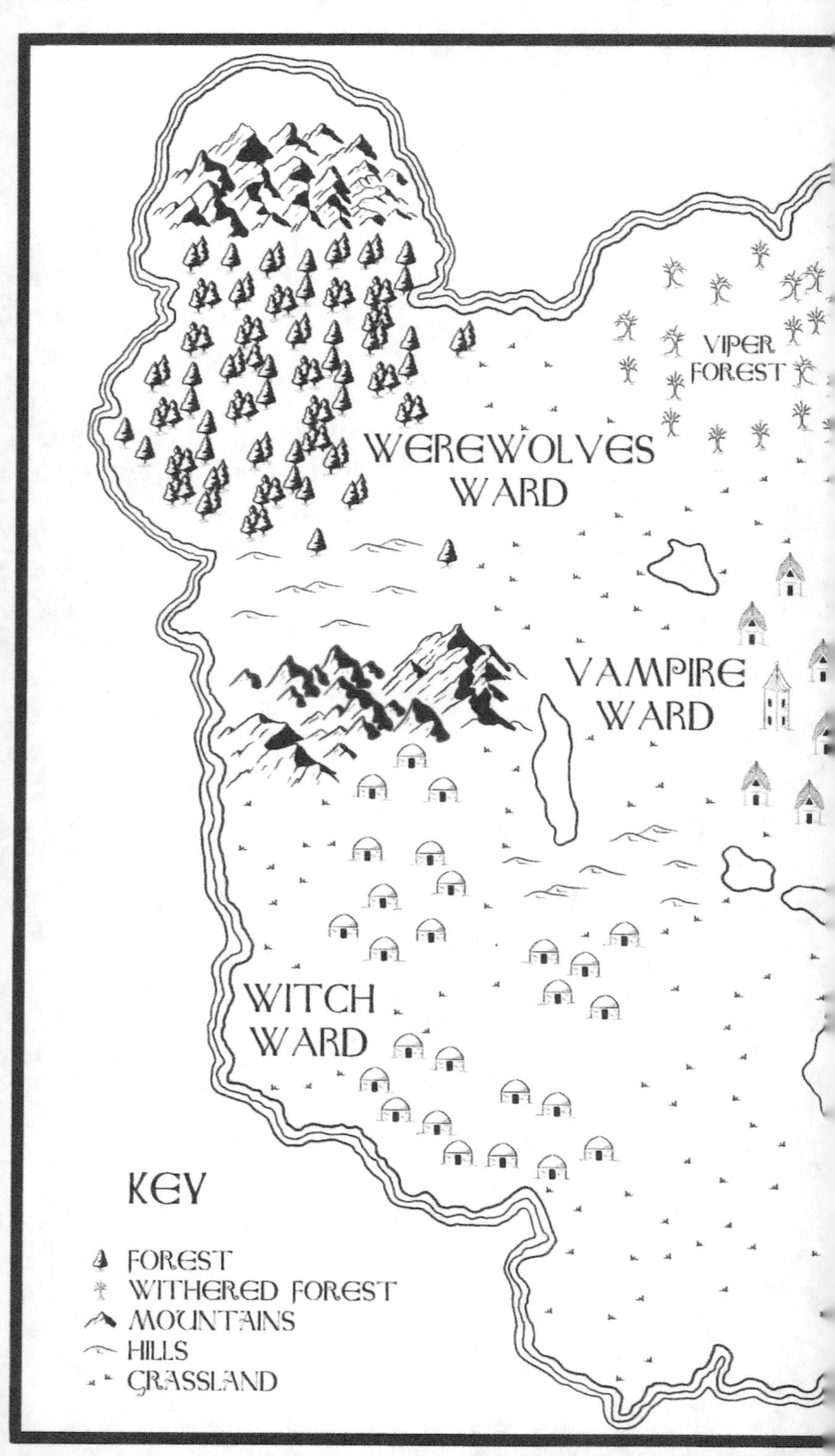

CRUEL QUEEN

COVER DESIGN - BY HANG LE
Drawings - Macarena Ceballos/Mikki
Editor - Swish Editing, Ink Machine Editing & Nice Girl, Naughty Edits

Kingdoms are broken.

The world has shifted.

We are not the same as we once were.

The queen is no longer the queen, but I am expected to take her place. The tricky part is I'm not sure I want that responsibility. My heart screams for Death while he stays as far away as possible, believing in the prophecy, whereas I believe in us.

But sometimes, that simply isn't enough.

The real question now is... what do I do?

Chapter One

"I know you can hear me." A frustrated scream rips from my lips. "Grim, I know you can hear me, you asshole." My foot makes contact with a rock, and I swear as pain shoots through my toes.

Fuck.

Shit.

Yeah, swearing is the new me.

I am a new me.

For the last few months, I've been living with the wolves, staying out of everyone's way, and simply doing my own thing.

And I haven't seen Grim since.

The Angel of Death.

The one man—if you want to call him that—who

has ever made me want someone has evaded me at every turn.

And I know he visits. I felt it the first night when one of the wolves died. I simply knew he was there.

But enough is enough.

"Grim, I swear to God... if you don't get your ass down here right now, I will..." I try to think of something to piss him off. But I feel like dying would be what's needed, so I try a different tact. "I'll kiss Bronik."

He doesn't need to know that I won't actually do it.

Bronik... well, Bronik is handsome and fun to be around. There is an attraction, for sure. He helps me practice magic and strengthens my fighting abilities and skills. Basically, he is... nice. And my favorite thing about Bronik is that he doesn't take.

Standing tall and absolutely delicious, Grim hasn't changed as he appears in front of me. His long, dark hair is tied back, and he's dressed in all black.

"Why must you test me?" are his first words, his tone deceiving, his expression unreadable. "I've told you... this *cannot* work."

"Yet here you stand." I feel his dark gaze wash over me—every inch of me.

"You cut your hair," he declares, and my hand subconsciously touches the strands. It's short. The cut sits above my shoulders. I disliked maintaining the length, so this was the easiest solution.

"Do you hate it?" I ask Grim, not knowing why I care if he likes it or not. He doesn't want me, but the problem is everything inside me wants him.

"No, it's more..."—he pauses, as if he is trying to find the right word—"... you."

I smile as he glances over my shoulder and then focuses back on me. "You stayed with the wolves, even knowing Viper is on his way."

"The vampires hold the castle. What am I meant to do?" I ask, with a slight shake of my head. "I'm just one girl."

I see him take a deep breath and then sigh in frustration. "You are anything but *just* a girl."

"I'm still learning," I reply with an exhale, sure my feelings are showing on my face.

"Lies. You know how to use your powers."

"I need more time."

"You won't have it."

Then he's gone.

And I stomp my foot like he can see me.

I head back to the house that Tanya and I share. Tatiana is with John as much as humanly possible, and the pack has started to warm to her. Well, somewhat. Most of the women despise her, but luckily the men accept John's choice.

"You ran off to scream at the sky again?" Melvon is standing there, and I stop in my tracks. I poke my tongue out at him, which makes him chuckle and keep walking. Melvon wasn't welcome here, but John let that slide since he helped save our lives. He tends to stay away from all the other wolves and does his own thing out near the boundary.

Bronik comes and goes. He shows up to train, then *poof*. Gone.

"Talia." I stop as Tatiana approaches me. She grips my wrist and starts pulling me hard.

"Hey, that hurts." I attempt to tug free, but she's not having it.

She keeps pulling until we approach the tree line, and then she sits on the ground, her hands sinking into the earth–her being an Earth witch and all.

"Tatiana?" I squat down, so I am at her level. Her eyes are closed, and she's humming something. "Tatiana," I try again.

"Ohhh, Wings, how I have missed you."

I stand quickly and spin to Valefar, who's now standing before me. He probes me with his black eyes before they fall to my sister on the ground. "You called?"

Shocked, I whip my head to look down at her.

"You didn't call him, did you?" I ask. *There's no way.*

4

"Oh, but she did. Sister dearest is in a predicament," Valefar says.

My eyes shift to hers once more.

"I've tried everything, and nothing has worked," Tatiana states with a grimace.

"What are you talking about?"

"I'm pregnant," she replies, dropping a bomb that has my mouth agape before I right myself. "I don't want to be," she adds. "But I can't tell John that."

"So why is Valefar here? You know he's a demon, right? I mean, you can still think straight?"

Tatiana stands and rolls her eyes. "Yes, it's new. The baby doesn't even have a heartbeat yet, but I guess I conceived last week."

"The perks of being a witch," Valefar comments.

We tend to know when we're pregnant, and John will know the minute he can hear a second heartbeat.

"You want an elixir," Valefar states.

"Nope, no way. Speak to John first," I tell her as tears run down her cheeks.

"Viper is almost at the castle. You know as well as I do that he's powerful enough to get in. Do you really think he will let you live? Only the person with ultimate power holds the throne, and you are that person."

"So you're saying you don't want a baby because of

me?" I ask, my hand raising to my chest as I step back, horrified at the thought.

She shakes her head. "No, I want to protect you, and I can't do that if I'm fat!" she screams.

Valefar laughs at her outburst.

"John!" I shout as loudly as I can, calling him to our side.

Valefar disappears, leaving Tatiana and me.

"Why did you do that?"

"Because you'll make an excellent mother. Don't let me stop you. That's not something I would ever want on my conscience."

John runs over, his hands gliding over Tatiana to check for injuries before he glances at me. "What happened?" he asks, then starts sniffing the air. "A demon was here."

Shit! I forgot how good his sense of smell is.

"Tatiana wants to talk to you. I'm just going to..." I start to back away, when Grim appears again, directly in my path this time. He reaches out and captures me, holding me to him before we disappear.

I know where we are as soon as we reappear.

Our place.

Everything is so pristine. I step away from his grip and walk to the water, the same water we fucked in. Where I realized we could never be. How much I want us to be eats me alive every day.

"Why am I here?" I ask. When I turn back, those silver eyes are locked on me. "Grim?"

"You are here because I want you here."

"And why is that?" I push a little more. When he doesn't answer, I start to remove my clothes. The sun is setting, and the weather is warm. When I'm down to my panties with my back still to him, I slide them down incredibly slow, bending over just to taunt him. I can feel his stare penetrating through me. Standing, I glance back at him over my shoulder. His face is strained, and his lips are pressed in a thin line as I continue toward the water.

"The last woman I took died with a man's head between her legs." He looks at me, confused. I pause as my feet hit the cold water. "Do you enjoy that? Having a man between your legs? She did. Is this something a woman wants?" he asks.

"I've never had one there," I answer truthfully. "I've had sex. But foreplay..." I shake my head.

"Foreplay?" he asks.

"Yes. Like how I gripped your cock and stroked it before you went inside of me. You know... foreplay."

"And women like this... stroking?" he asks.

"I heard it's amazing with a tongue." I shrug before submerging myself in the water, then return to the surface and shake my head. "I may very well try it soon." I lie back in the water and float, enjoying the calming sensation. He says something, but I don't hear him, as my ears are in the water.

Then, before I know it, hands grip me, and I'm lifted before being carried to the sand, where Grim lays me down on his shirt.

"Grim?" I say his name, waiting for an answer. I lift up and touch his face, his eyes locking onto mine, and I lean in. "Kiss me, please."

"We should be going. We've done well. This can't happen."

I quickly get to my knees and reach for him anyway, slamming my lips to his. He doesn't kiss me back at first, just lets my lips move over his until I go to pull away. Then he grips me and slides his tongue between my lips.

Ecstasy.

There is no other word.

I don't think in this lifetime I will ever experience a kiss like ours, a touch like we share, or anything remotely like what we have.

I can only hope I do, because I know we'll never be.

He is the Angel of Death.

And I am a witch.

The two don't work.

The two can't work.

And it is devastating.

Yet we keep lying to ourselves, as we are right now.

Held tight in his embrace, his hands slide to my bare ass, gripping my flesh with strength that makes me moan. As his tongue caresses mine, he pushes me back, but holds me so I don't fall. I lie beneath him as he hovers above me, our lips meeting again. But then he's pulling away much too suddenly, breaking our kiss before I get my fill.

"We have to stop meeting like this." Grim freezes, and I smile. "Talia, Viper is requesting a meeting with you." I turn my head and see Bronik looming behind us.

"Leave," Grim says, and his voice holds a threat that I wasn't aware of before this moment.

"Why must you return? You know the rules," Bronik says to Grim before he disappears.

Grim's silver eyes fall on me. "I hate him," he growls and goes to stand, but I wrap my legs around his waist and hold him to me. He could easily break my hold without effort, but he stays put.

"About that foreplay..." I say, wiggling under him.

"You have to go."

"Why, because Bronik said so? I think not." I lean up and kiss his lips before I pull back. "So, who should start first? I'm not averse to practicing my skills on you. You can tell me if I am any good." I smile. He manages to smile back at me, but I know what he's about to do

9

—he's about to stop this before it's even begun. So I slide my hands between us and straight into his pants.

That's what a normal person does, right? Probably not.

His head drops, and he looks between our bodies, where my hand is currently gripping his cock. The fun thing about an Angel is they don't wear underwear.

"I dream of you," I say as I continue stroking him. "In those dreams, I'm doing this while you are..." His mouth lands on my neck, and he kisses and sucks his way down until he gets to my naked breasts. He takes one in his mouth while his hand pulls my hand free from his cock. As he works his way down my body, I lie there, staring up at the blue sky, wondering if this is what heaven is like.

"No," Grim replies to my thoughts. "Heaven is you." His mouth touches the spot just above my center, my back arching in response. He kisses it softly before his tongue moves farther down and swipes at my clit. I squeal, and he pauses to make sure I'm okay before he does it again, eliciting another squeal and whimper at the sensation.

I cover my mouth as he starts a slow and steady pattern with his own, circling and exploring. He does it like he does everything in life—with precision and excellence. He sure is gifted for someone who isn't experienced in the sex department.

"Finger. Put a finger inside me."

He does, continuing his movements with his lips and tongue. Grim's finger pumps in and out of me, while his mouth devours me as if I belong to him.

Do I?

I don't even want to know the answer to that.

I'm not sure I'm ready.

He pushes a second finger in, and his other hand presses down on my lower stomach as he licks, pumps, and delights me in every single way possible.

Foreplay.

I like it.

My hands find the sand, and I try to grip it, but it falls through my fingers as I come. When I finally stop writhing, so does Grim. He slides up my body until his face is in line with mine.

"I think that was my favorite," he tells me. I can't help the laugh that leaves me. "What?" he questions.

"Wait until I use my mouth on you." I wink at him.

He stands, looking down and holding out my clothes in his hand.

"You have to stop calling me."

Goddamnit! All happiness is sucked out of the moment at his words.

I reach for my clothes and put them on with jerky movements. My frustration clear.

"This was our last goodbye?" I ask, feeling more despondent than I did before seeing him again.

"Yes." He touches my hand, and before I can blink, we're back where he took me from. He doesn't say a word as he disappears.

And I think he took a piece of my heart with him.

Chapter Two

"They've been in there for hours. Is it true? Is she pregnant?" Tanya asks. I shrug my shoulders, not sure if I should tell her or not. "Why does she tell you everything and not me? I'm closer in age," she whines.

Melvon comes into our small house carrying some bread.

Tanya's face instantly changes, and she offers him a smile before she takes it from him. "Thanks, Melvon."

She's been feeding him.

She thinks we don't know.

But Melvon and Tatiana are still connected. She knows the risk of feeding a vampire—our blood is addictive to them. While she has a crush, he looks at her as a meal.

Melvon's eyes fall on me.

"Bronik is here. He asked I fetch you so he doesn't intrude again... in case you are busy." I roll my eyes, get off the bed, and walk out with Tanya and Melvon following.

I spot Bronik straight away. He's standing with a group of shifters around him, all watching him closely.

Tatiana approaches, with John by her side. Her eyes find mine, and by the redness surrounding them, I can see she's been crying.

"Can we help you, Angel?" John says.

"Bronik," Bronik corrects him. "Or would you prefer I call you *dog* instead of John?" Tatiana lays a hand on John's shoulder to calm him. Bronik then addresses me. "Do you want to meet with him?"

"Who?" Tatiana asks, coming to stand next to me. "Who is he talking about, Talia?"

"Viper wants a meeting," I tell her.

"Hell no. That's what you said, right?" she asks, eyes wide.

"I haven't said no."

"It's best she goes so she can get a feel for him. He knows of her power. Everyone does. She is his competition... therefore, they should speak. Since he holds the castle now."

"He wants to kill her," Tatiana barks at Bronik.

"And I would not let that happen."

"If Viper wanted to, he could control you," Tatiana says.

"It's not that easy. He may be able to subdue me, but control... well, let's say that should not happen again."

"Unless he makes a deal with a demon," I utter.

Bronik stares at me intently, and I just shrug.

"Talia can't go. She is safer here," Tatiana adds. She's staying strong, but I can hear the pleading.

"She isn't safe anywhere, and you are a fool to believe so," Bronik replies.

"I'd watch who you call a fool," John warns.

Bronik doesn't even glance at him.

"He knows you don't want the crown. He wants to test you."

"Viper and his testing can go suck a vampire's dick." I cross my arms over my chest. "Last time I was tested, I had to kill one of his people. That was *not* fun."

"She isn't going," my sister reiterates.

"If he has the vampires, the forest, and the castle, you and this little pack of wolves won't be able to say no to him. He will rule how he wants to rule."

"I kind of don't care," I say, shrugging. "I'm over this world anyway." I offer him a smile.

"I assumed you wouldn't let a man get in your way. I see I was mistaken."

"A man?" Tanya says.

"Sorry, I misspoke. An Angel of Death."

"You've seen him?" Tatiana asks, her gaze snapping to mine.

I look up at Bronik, and he gives me a smirk.

"I have."

"You said he wouldn't come when you called," Tatiana states with her brows drawn together.

"He wouldn't—"

"Until he did," Bronik interjects.

"I don't particularly like you very much," I say to Bronik, narrowing my eyes.

"That's okay. I don't need you to like me for me to do my job."

"And what is that, exactly?"

"To put you on the throne, of course. Once you are there, the world will start to turn green, witches will thrive once again, wolves can run free into the forest, vampires will have their own nests, and humans will choose, if they wish, to give blood. This is the vision I was granted when I had to stay. I will help and do everything in my power to make it come true," Bronik announces.

"We won't be confined here any longer?" one of the women wolves asks. "We can go anywhere?"

My eyes swing back to her. She's young and one of the wolves who speaks to me without attitude.

"Yes. With Talia on the throne, the world will be a better place. How it's intended to be, and not how those with hunger see it."

"Talia." Tatiana touches my shoulder.

"You are keeping it?" I ask in a hushed voice. She smiles and nods her head as I lay a hand on her shoulder. "I'm happy for you, I am. But this—"

"You don't have to. We can stay here and protect what we can." And I believe her words, I do. I know she would die for me, for everyone here. Well, maybe not Bronik. But she would try.

I wrap my hands around her shoulders and pull her in for a hug.

"Good, you're staying," she says, rubbing my back. "Let's cook tonight."

"I hate cooking." I giggle, pulling away. Then I step closer to Bronik. "I'll see you soon, okay?" I smile.

Before Tatiana can say another word, Bronik's hand lands on my shoulder, and we are gone.

"Y ou can remove your hand now," I tell Bronik with a huff. He offers me a smirk, lifting his hand from my shoulder and checking around. I turn away from him and stare straight ahead.

Crystal Castle sits in front of us. It appears the

same—a Baroque theme with long-taloned gargoyles poised on top. The only thing that is different is it seems to have brought the forest with it. Trees are everywhere, and a lush, awe-inducing landscape surrounds the castle.

"Viper's doing," Bronik comments, leaving it at that as I look on. He reaches for my arm again, but I pull away.

"We can go in," I say, stepping away from him and heading toward the door. The last thing I want is to be forced back into that castle. My memories of that place are not pleasant, and I'm not sure I want to walk through those doors, even of my free own will. When I stare at it, all I see is the bad. Of how we were dragged here, of how I watched the queen take Patrick's life, and how his lifeless body lay in front of me. I've got this heavy weight on my shoulders, and the only thing I want to do is go back to that beach where Grim is and spend the rest of my days watching the water and stealing kisses. *Why can't I have that?*

The giant wooden door opens when we reach the castle. It's much the same as the last time I was here, with its pristine white walls and the chandelier hanging from the ceiling. The most obvious difference is the green, flowering plants crawling up the walls, turning it into Viper's own personal forest. Dare I say it feels homier than it used to, which is weird considering it is Viper who lives here.

"Awww, you came. I had my doubts."

"You had your doubts? Can you *not* see me anymore, Viper?" I tease, knowing he can because he is, after all, the last seer alive. The queen could not kill him because he had the forest, and she could not enter, as that was his domain.

"No, it seems you are lost to me." His words shock me, and I side-eye Bronik, who stands silently beside me. "Not quite sure why. So figured if I saw you again, maybe..." He saunters over to me, dressed much like he was the first time I met him, in a green coat, which seems to be made of leaves, diamonds decorating his body that show off how beautiful his dark skin is, and white eyes that could seemingly eviscerate you with one look. I've seen many different colored eyes, but his are the only ones to ever make me shiver.

Viper's hand lifts to my hair.

"You cut it," he declares, lightly tugging on a strand.

"What made that obvious, the length?" I roll my eyes and he flicks my hair before he steps back.

"You are stronger. This is why I cannot see you any longer."

"I feel like I should give you an award, but I'm not inclined to." I smile at him, but it's not a nice one.

"And you have a much larger attitude. Tell me... was it when you sliced the queen's neck that made you grow some balls?"

I clench my jaw at his words.

The door behind him opens and Cinitta steps into the room. She isn't in her other form. Today she is in her most beautiful one. Her long, violet hair cascades down her back, and her violet eyes find mine. A smile begins to form on her lips, but she thinks better of it, and her mouth thins into a straight line.

"Hmm... you're happy to see Cinitta but not me. That's a shame since I helped you rescue your sister," Viper points out, smiling eerily.

"You mean where I had to use blood to get across the barrier?" I ask him.

"Yes, about that. I see your wolf is no longer with you. Was it him you used?"

I don't bother answering him. He isn't worthy of my time. Instead, I ask, "What is it you requested me for?"

Viper tuts and strides away. I stay where I am until he pins me with a look over his shoulder. "Follow, dear."

I do as he asks, with Bronik close behind me. I walk past Cinitta, but she refuses to look at me, keeping her head down.

As we move right past *that* room, the one that

holds so many nightmares, Viper doesn't even flinch. I glance back at Bronik to see him staring at it the same way I am.

With disgust.

Revulsion.

We head into the dining room, noting the table the queen used is no longer here. In its place sits a round table with a vase filled with roses situated in the middle.

"We need to discuss business. Sit, sit." He pulls out his chair, and I do the same, and the two of us take our seats. He smiles and clicks his fingers, and someone comes out and puts a cup of tea in front of me, followed by some treats. I see the chocolate, and my mouth starts watering, but I make no move to touch any of it.

Viper may be acting kind right now.

But we all know he is anything but kind.

"What is it you wanted to discuss?" I ask.

"Drink. I promise it's not poison."

"I'll pass," I say, pushing the glass teacup away.

"As you wish," he says, lifting his cup to his lips and taking a sip before he places it down and opens his mouth again. "You do not aspire to be queen." He levels me with a look that's hard to ignore. "I may not see you anymore, but I know this. You would have taken the castle if you did."

He's right. I would have. Instead, I retreated and left it unattended, and the vampires took it. Unfortunately, then Viper easily snatched it from their control.

"So that makes me believe you do not understand how the world works. We need a leader, and this world needs order. The vampires started to kill all humans, feeding on them as if there is a world of them somewhere else. The witches put up their own spell to keep said vampires out. Which, if I might say, it's about time. Have you been back to the witches?"

"No."

"You should go. They are your kind."

"And what of yours?" I ask him.

"You know the answer to this..." He pauses for a moment. "They're all dead." His fingers tap on the table. "It's why I took over the castle. The one who holds the ultimate power must. And between you and me, my dear, that *is* me."

"You think you have more power than me?" I laugh and throw my head back. When I glance back at him, he's watching me with an unmoving gaze. One that would have most cowering. "You do not, Viper, have more power than me. Tell me, can you kill me if you touch me?" I ask as I stand.

I feel Bronik's eyes on me, but I don't even bother glancing his way. Stepping around the table until I reach Viper's side, I touch his shoulder. And the minute I do, I begin siphoning his powers. It's a light touch—I don't intend to kill him—but the minute I taste it, I'm hungry, and my other hand lifts and lands on his shoulder as well. He tastes like the most invigorating breath of air and everything vibrantly green. What an odd flavor. Suddenly, I'm lifted into the air and thrown back, my body slamming into the white floor. But I just lie there with not a care in the world.

What a beautiful power.

Lifting my head, I lock eyes with Viper. And I know, I just know, my eyes are white right now.

"It's refreshing to see what you see."

And before I know it, something hits me, not physically, but mentally. My body caves into itself, and a loud scream echoes through the room.

What I don't realize is that scream comes from me.

Chapter Three

Cinitta and her sister are hovering over me when I open my eyes. Gone is her violet hair, and in its place is scaly skin and fire. Managing to sit up, I realize Viper is standing a short distance away with a look of revulsion etched all over his face.

"How dare you?" he seethes.

"I can see you, Viper. I can see the deal you made," I say quietly. "Valefar," I whisper. And in the next instant, Valefar is standing in front of me. He checks around until his eyes find the sisters on either side of me, then he offers me a smile.

"I see you are still in trouble, Wings. Must run in the family." He winks.

"You made a deal with Viper?" I accuse. I don't need him to confirm the question because I can see it.

"Oh, that small thing. People are so hungry for power. For a power like yours, to be precise, Wings, but we just can't give them that."

"Demon." Valefar turns to Viper. "Get out of my house."

"Tsk, tsk," Valefar says and looks back at me.

"You must get this everywhere you go," I say to him, not curtailing my smile.

"Except you, Wings. You seem to welcome me." He turns back to Viper. "This is not your house."

"The queen is dead."

"No, she stands right here." Valefar steps back and waves a hand in my direction. "It seems she has had a taste of your power. Tell me, Wings"—he brings his attention back to me—"was it delicious?"

I nod my head and lick my lips.

"That's because it's laced with mine."

I'm shocked at his words. "I thought deals were beneath you."

"Not this deal," he replies, and before anyone can utter another word, he is gone.

"Cinitta." I step closer and reach for her. As soon as I make contact with her skin, the fire goes out, and she is back to her true form. "You don't have to serve him," I tell her. "He's lying. The deal with your mother is long dead."

She pulls my hand away, and the fire bursts back to life.

"That won't work," Viper states simply, sounding bored. "But you know what does work?" He snaps his fingers, and pain radiates through me instantly. Every fiber of my being is engulfed in an indescribable agony. I drop to the floor, my hands cooling at the feel of the marble beneath me.

I hear his steps as he comes closer, and I can do nothing to stop what happens next.

"Portals."

Another snap of his fingers, and I'm falling.

Falling with no end in sight.

* * *

No one has ever come back from a portal. It's well known that there is no return once you go through one.

I should have expected something like this from Viper. I mean, I did piss him off. *But a portal?* Asshole.

My back slams into the ground, my head throbbing on contact, and I must remember I need to move.

I don't know this world.

This world is not mine.

Only a few have the power to open portals. And it seems somehow Viper is now one of those few. Is this the place where everyone goes that disobeyed the queen, or did she just kill them?

I don't even know for sure.

Another thing, this world is not for Angels or demons. So I can't even conjure Valefar if I try. Opening my eyes, I look up to see stars, indicating that it's nighttime. At least, as far as I can tell. My head is throbbing, and I think I kinked something in the back of my neck.

A distant noise becomes louder—it sounds like a bird. But not just a small bird chirping, more like a flock, maybe?

Managing to pull myself up and turn over, I crawl to the nearest tree where I can hide. As soon as I reach it, instant relief floods through me.

We thought that portals went to hell. No one really knew where you went because you just kind of... went.

Sitting with my back to the tree, I take in my surroundings. The stars shine brightly, making everything visible. Trees are everywhere I look, but they aren't your average trees like the ones seen in Cardia. These have purple and pink flowers blossoming. I rub my eyes to make sure I see correctly, and sure enough, I am. Managing to stand, I turn around. The tree I'm leaning against is also pink and purple, and beneath my feet is lush green grass.

Everything here is so...

... dare I say, *beautiful*.

This can't be Hell, can it?

The birds that were chirping before stop. And it seems everything goes quiet, hauntingly so.

The only thing I hear is the gentle sound of water lapping against a shore. Following the sound, I walk past the eye-catching trees and find a lake. Bending down, I go to put my hands in it to wash my face.

"I wouldn't do that if I were you."

My head shoots up at the sound of the voice, and I stop. Sitting on the other side of the lake is a man who's dressed in what appears to be an all-black suit. But it's not your average suit, more like a bodice top with long sleeves, and trousers that are form-fitting, but not quite as tight as a woman's.

"Why?" I ask.

"This is sacred water. You are not permitted to touch it." My eyes go wide at his words. He turns away from me and bites into what seems to be an apple. I stare at him, taking in his features. His hair is short, brushed back to perfection, and the color of a deep blue with hints of lighter brown strokes. His features are prominent, and his jaw is impeccably strong.

Dare I say it?

This man is stunning.

His eyes find mine, and they slice through me, and I almost feel bad for staring. *Almost.* He bites into the apple again as he studies me before he offers me a wink, then poof, he's gone.

I stare at the spot where he was, bewildered.

What just happened?

And then I hear footsteps, several of them, coming in my direction. I manage to move but not quickly enough. I'm suddenly surrounded by men in blue uniforms, each of them holding some kind of weapon as they all stare at me, and all of them appear the same.

"Invader," one of them sneers.

I look around, not sure what is going on, or what to expect, but knowing whatever it is can't be good. A hand reaches out to grab me, and I react quickly, putting fire to the hand that touches me. His sleeve lights up, and he hisses, as does everyone else.

"Witch," someone snarls.

And before I can say or do anything else, I'm overcome by something—not physically, but more like a spell.

And the last thing I see is a flash of blue.

"She's from that world." My head is groggy, but I can make out their words.

"You don't know that."

"But she is, my lord. Look at her. She isn't from

here." Footsteps come closer, then stop. I hear someone breathing right in front of me.

"You can open your eyes now. I know you're awake."

I do as the voice asks, and when I do, I see him leaning over in front of me, a smile attached to his lips as he stares down at me. It's the man from the lake, dressed pretty much the same way he was when I first saw him.

"How did you use that spell on me?" I ask, because most spells have been known not to work on me. I always assumed I was immune. Unless a demon was involved, that is.

"Your magic is different from our magic. Over the years, your magic has been diluted, where ours has only grown."

"Diluted?" I sit up, my interest piqued. He remains crouched down in front of me, and his eyes, the color of a light blue sky, gaze back at me. I wonder if they look the same under the night sky.

"Yes. You let bloodsuckers and other things dilute your line, whereas ours is still pure."

What does he mean by *theirs is pure*? As I sit there, trying to take in everything he's saying, he stands to tower over me.

"The spell should have lasted longer on you, though." He clicks his tongue. "You are a witch, correct?" There is no need to deny it, so I give him a slight nod of my head. He offers me his hand, and I glance at it, wondering what the trick is. "I will not harm you." He pauses. "Yet." His voice sounds like a promise—a deadly promise. I'm not sure if I should walk into it or not. I have no other choice, though, not until I can work out how to get back to my sisters.

I take his offered hand and pull myself up. When I'm standing, I see we're in an outdoor castle that's open to the elements. The floor is made of old marble peeking through the same lush green grass and blossoming trees I admired earlier.

"Levy will show you to your room to get changed. I would like you to accompany me to dinner." It's then I see guards surround us, but the woman who steps out and bows to the man makes me realize he must be some kind of authority figure. A king, perhaps? But he doesn't wear a crown. Levy, who offers me a kind smile, waves her small arm in the opposite direction from which I am facing. She is dressed in blue, the same as the guards, but she wears a casual free flowing dress, not the military-like uniform of the men.

I turn away from the mystery man and follow Levy. When we get to the exit, I look back to see him watching me. He offers me a smile, and I give him one back, not sure why, and then continue after Levy.

"Where are we?" I ask. She turns her nose up at me over her shoulder. "Well, okay. Rude."

"I am not rude. You are rude. How dare you come into our home."

"If I remember correctly, it wasn't my choice."

She grunts and walks into a dark hallway lined with doors. She stops when we get to one flanked by two guards and looks back at me. "This is your room. You have a dress inside. Wear it and get rid of"—she pauses, looking at my clothes with a pinched mouth— "*that*." She waves her hand at me and stalks off.

One of the guards opens the door to let me in, but I hesitate, unsure I should go in. It's a gorgeous room, more so than the queen's, which is saying a lot because she had the prettiest room I had ever seen.

In the middle is an oversized bed with four poles, all draped with the same pink and purple flowers from outside. I slowly approach and run my fingers along the sheets—they're silk. Sitting on it, I check around. It has its own vanity, a closed wooden cupboard that is engraved with animals, and a door I'm not sure where it leads. We don't have many animals left in Cardia, but I've seen pictures of them before in books I wasn't supposed to read. And the one animal I wish I had the most was a dog or maybe a lion.

Standing, I shift to open the cupboard and find a pink dress hanging inside. Fingering the material, I find that it is silk as well. It's the only dress in here, so I pull it from the cupboard and carry it with me as I head to the other door. When I push it open, there's a large bathing area filled with an array of colorful flowers, and it smells divine. I have never smelled anything like the aroma in here before.

This new world is filled with so much wonder.

And yet ours struggles in so many ways.

It's sad.

Maybe even tragic when I think about it.

Walking to the already filled tub, I put my hand in the water and find it's warm. Undressing and placing the dress down on the ornate chair in the corner, I climb in, immediately sighing at how good it feels.

And when I put my head under the water, I close my eyes and think of him.

Death.

Chapter Four

L evy is waiting with her hand on her hip when I step out. Though still wearing a blue dress, this one is fancier. More dramatic. The pink dress I wear clings to my body and shows every curve. I've never worn something like this, and I can't decide if I like the way it feels to be on display.

"Follow, witch," she commands, then disappears. I do as she says, my bare feet slapping against the floor. The shoes I had on were so dirty I was afraid they might ruin the dress, so I decided not to bother.

When I step out of the room, I spot her down the hallway and try to keep up, but she moves quickly as she takes a corner. When I reach it, I don't see her, just another large room. Stepping inside, I look around, when she suddenly pops out from behind me, tapping me on the shoulder and eliciting a scream.

"Jumpy." She all but laughs.

I would very much like to set her on fire.

"Where are we going?"

"Dinner, of course. With the king."

"King?" I ask.

"Yes, you met him. Keep up, witch."

"Are you not a witch?" I inquire. I actually don't expect her to answer, but she does.

"No, I am better than a witch." I scoff, which makes her turn around and pin me with her eyes. "You think you are better than me?"

"I said nothing of the sort."

"All of your kind who fall down and invade our world are the same... half breeds with hardly any power and thrown out of your own world to annoy us in ours."

"Tell a girl how you really feel," I reply to her cattiness.

She steps closer and gets in my face.

"If you touch me, I will *not* be held responsible for what I do," I warn her.

She smirks, but it's not a lovely smirk. It's more of a *try it, witch*.

"Levy." A guard says her name, but she ignores him. "The king is waiting."

"Yes, Levy, we don't want to disappoint the king." I show her a sarcastic smile.

She spins on her heel, whipping her long hair in my face, and goes through the side door that she popped out from. I follow her into an elaborately decorated dining area. A waterfall quietly flows down the back wall, with small silver birds perched around it. They are known to flock to those who are powerful. I figured they were made-up stories, as I have never seen one in real life. But wow!

"You seem taken by my peachies," a voice echoes next to me.

"Peachies," I repeat, stepping farther into the room. I keep walking until I reach the water, where the birds are perched on a branch... just sitting there.

The rumour states that if a peachie wants, it can take life and hold it. When it's time, it can choose to give that life to someone who is worthy. I turn back, and he is standing next to me, his dark hair slicked back, and he's wearing a gray suit similar to the one he wore earlier. It shows his form and how strong he is. "Are they yours?" I ask.

"I am king," he whispers.

I should have guessed.

I had my suspicions, but wasn't sure.

"Can I touch one?" You have to ask permission to touch them, as it's the owner's responsibility to care for them once they choose you.

"I..." Just as he goes to speak, one of the silver birds flies to me and lands on my shoulder. I giggle as it makes a weird sound and makes itself comfortable on me. "Very strange," he adds. I turn my head toward him and find him staring at me, his brow furrowing almost imperceptibly with curiosity. "They are attracted to power."

"I know." I smile and look back at the bird. I offer it my hand, and it climbs into it willingly.

"Sir." I hear her voice but choose not to pay her any attention because she clearly isn't talking to me. "Dinner is served."

"Thank you, Levy."

"Do you prefer to be called sir?" I ask him, stroking the bird's feathers as it sits quietly in my hand.

"Maxilliam is my name. Those who serve me call me sir or king, but you can call me Maxilliam." I nod at his words.

"I'm Talia, but you can call me Talia." I offer him a genuine smile, and his lips quirk in response.

"Talia. A beautiful name."

"Thank you. Though, I always preferred my sister's name."

"You have a sister?"

"Yes, I have two. But the eldest is named Tatiana. It has a nice ring to it, don't you think?"

"Yes, but Talia suits you. Come, let's eat." I lift the bird, place it back on the branch with others, then turn around to face him. He offers me his elbow, and I take it. "You misplaced your shoes?" he asks, looking amused.

"No, I didn't think the ones I had on went with such a beautiful dress."

When we reach the table, Levy is seated directly next to where the king would sit. She glances down when we approach as someone pulls out his chair and mine. I drop my arm from his and sit as he does. The food follows, and I observe with wonder in my eyes as it's all laid out in front of me. All over the table are loaves of bread, rice in weird shapes, green cakes, pink cakes, chocolate, salads, and fruit.

"Are we expecting anyone else, or just us?" I ask Maxilliam.

"I figured for tonight you would be more comfortable with just us, but usually I eat with my guards, and Levy, of course."

I glance at Levy to see her smiling at Maxilliam.

"Is she your wife?" I ask, and Levy blushes at my words.

"No, she is not. I have not taken a wife."

I look at Levy. "But you hope to be his wife?" I ask her.

"Yes."

I nod at her honesty before I turn back to Maxilliam. "That's nice. I'm sure you will make a lovely couple." I smile, then jump right into the only question circling my mind. "Now, how do I leave this place?"

Maxilliam reaches for some food and plates it before he answers me. "We have not discovered a way to get to your world."

"Fuck!" I swear, and my head drops into my hands.

"*Fuck?* What is that?" Maxilliam asks.

I lift my head and stare at him, not really knowing how to answer, so I go with, "It's a word to describe my frustration right now," I reply, taking a breath. "I can give you a list of words, though most of them are bad and probably should be said only in private."

"Yes, please." He nods with interest. "You will stay here."

"Am I free to explore?" I need to find a way out of here and back to my sisters.

"Yes, but only with a guard. As you are unfamiliar with this land, it's best to have someone with you at all times. I can always assign Levy to you."

Oh, hell no! Both Levy and I straighten.

"No, a guard will do."

"So tell me... you are a witch, correct?" he asks.

"Yes..." I pause before I continue, wondering if I even should. "Do you hold powers?" He offers me a smirk before I feel my chair being lifted into the air. I turn around and see no one is there, and when I look at the king, he smiles before gently placing me back down.

"You could say I do."

"And you?" Levy ignores me and eats her food.

"Levy is a changer. She can change her appearance to be whom she wishes." Maxilliam taps her hand, and as the fork lifts to her mouth, she changes into me, dressed exactly the same.

"Wow." I lean in, cringing. "Is my hair that bad?" I touch my own hair and pat it down. She shakes her head and returns to who she was—the change taking place quickly.

"We possess a lot of powers the witches hold, even the seers that you have." Maxilliam tells me.

"You have seers?" I ask, confused.

"Yes, many. They came from your land." I glance to Levy at his words as I sit back, letting that information sink in. The only seer left in my world is Viper. *Stupid Viper.* I thought they were all killed, but it seems I was mistaken.

"Do you get a lot of people from where I am from?" I ask.

"Only what your queen sends through," Maxilliam states.

"Our queen is dead," I declare.

He sits back in his seat, lays his hands on the table, and studies me. "Dead, you say?"

I nod my head.

"Interesting. How did you get here?"

"A seer."

"A seer?" he questions. "They don't possess the ability to open a portal."

"One with demon magic can," I inform.

He says nothing, so I reach for some food and start eating.

A few minutes of quietness follow before he states, "You are strong. How did he manage to get you?"

I take a bite of the chocolate cake and instantly regret it. I know when I go back, I'll be dreaming of foods like this. Wishing I could have every lavish bite.

"Talia."

I look up to see both Levy and Maxilliam watching me.

"Sorry, what did you say?"

"How did this seer manage to get you?"

"I was distracted," I offer, not hiding my aggravation at the memory.

"Distractions are not warranted here."

"Why?"

He leans forward, eyes boring into mine. "Because people die."

"From?"

Levy scoffs as she chews on a piece of fruit.

"We have things in this world that are different from yours. Compared to what we used to be, we are dwindling, not what we once were. The darkness takes and takes, and not even I can stop it."

"The darkness?" I ask.

"Yes, it's what you call a figure, but these figures are made up of memories that lie and trick you. Once one of these figures gets to you, it will invade and suck the soul straight from your body. They are called yorks."

"You can't stop them?"

"No, we have never been able to."

"But you are powerful, correct? You have the birds." I glance back at the beautiful silver birds.

"Indeed, I am."

"I need to get back home," I tell him. "I can't stay here."

"Unless you can conjure a portal, Talia, you are staying, whether you want to or not." He pushes his chair backward and stands. I feel his eyes still on me, but I'm trying to sort through my knowledge. *Is there any way I can create a portal?* I mean, I've never really tried. *Is it hard? How hard can it be?* I hear his footsteps as he leaves, and when I turn back, Levy is smiling across the table from me.

"What?"

"Nice way to annoy our king."

"*Your* king," I say.

"No, *our* king. You are in *our world*, and if you choose to be disobedient, I will throw you to the yorks myself." She pushes her chair back and exits the same way Maxilliam left.

Chapter Five
TATIANA

Hands.

Hands that I dream about touch my body and move me, so I am lying on my back as he hovers over me. His hands skim and caress my stomach before his lips touch me there. I've had sex before John, but nothing compares to him and who he is. John is everything to me, just as my sisters are. I'm not sure how it happened, but it did, and I don't regret it.

He makes every inch of me come alive. As if he was born to make me feel this way only for him.

He tells me he was.

That it's his job to be that for me, that he was made to love me.

I admit I fought it at first—it was not the time to fall in love. It was anything but. But he just kept showing up, and soon that led to a kiss, followed by his hands, followed by...

Well, he sure knows how to please me, that's for sure.

And now I'm having a baby with him. I have no doubt he will be the best father imaginable, but it scares me to think of bringing life into this world when it's so broken.

But that's selfish, right? I'm not really sure.

His soft kisses linger until he grips the waistband of my pants, and I lift my hips for him to slide them off. He does so effortlessly, as he does everything when it involves me.

He knows how to calm me when needed.

How to reassure me when I'm worried.

I never thought in this life I would be in love with someone, not in this world, at least. It's all so dark and depressing.

I was raised to look after my sisters, and now I don't do that any longer. Instead, I help John with the wolves. Some of them still don't like me, but that's okay. I don't need their approval.

"Fuck, I love you!" he growls out the words as his mouth descends between my legs. I open them wider as his tongue slides in. He licks and tastes me like I am his favorite meal. I believe I am because he tells me so. When my hands are gripping my breasts, and I come, he slides his finger out of me and crawls back up my body. John leans down and kisses my mouth with a passion I feel all the way to my toes. I taste myself, but most of all, I taste him.

"We're having a baby," he says as he slides into me. My back arches as he does, and he kisses me again. "You are going to be the best mother." I want to tell him that I'm not sure how to be, but I keep my lips sealed as I feel him thrusting inside me.

Sex wasn't that enjoyable before, but now...

Holy shit on a brick.

I could open my legs and let him between them each and every day.

Starting with his mouth.

Followed by his cock.

Then back that up with his tongue circling my nipple.

The most attractive part about John is that he never, not ever, looks at anyone the way he looks at me.

I hope my sisters can have the same thing one day, but I'm concerned about Talia. Her love for Death will go nowhere good.

It can't.

It's impossible.

He is death, after all.

My hands lift and scrape down his back as I take him in deeper. I feel the build-up again, and a scream rips through my throat as John moves his hips faster and faster.

"That's my good girl," he says when I come. He kisses my forehead and then proceeds to kiss each breast as he releases inside of me.

"I love you," I whisper.

"I know," is all he says back.

Believe it or not, I say the words more than him, but he shows it ten times more than me. To him, love is not a word—it's in your actions. And his actions speak louder than any words ever could.

As soon as he lies down beside me, his hand comes to rest on my stomach, where he draws lazy circles.

"Witch or wolf?" I ask him.

"Both," he answers.

"She could be one and not the other."

"She?" he questions.

"Yes, she." I smile. "We Halaba girls seem to produce girls if you haven't noticed."

"Maybe that cycle will be broken."

"Maybe," I reply, not believing it.

A knock sounds at the door. I stand and reach for John's shirt before heading to answer. Bronik appears in the doorway as I pull it open, his face solemn, and his stance strong. But when I look behind him, I don't see my sister.

"Where is she?" I ask, pushing past him.

He moves to let me through, and I scan the area for Talia.

"Viper sent her through a portal."

I swing back around at his words. "What did you just say?" I scream at him. He goes to repeat himself, but I cut him off with my hand pressed to his mouth. "You told her to go to him. This was *your plan*," I accuse. "It's *your fault*!"

"Angel, what did you do?" John comes running out of the house and immediately to my side, his hand settling on my back. Usually, when he touches me, a part of me eases. Not this time, though. Now I am full of rage, and the Angel standing in front of me is my target. Just as I go to drop to the floor, he disappears.

"Asshole," I swear. "We need a portal," I tell John. "We need to find a portal."

"For what?" he questions.

"Viper sent Talia through one. How do I call Death? How does she do it?" I dig my hands into my hair and start pulling at it. John gently untangles my fingers from the knotted locks.

"Calm down, and let's think."

"Think? *Think*?" I throw my head back and laugh. "My sister was sent through a portal! I told her not to go see him. I knew Viper was a snake, and I was proven right."

"You are always right, my love." I swing my head

around to him and see Melvon approaching, drawn by my raging emotions. We are still connected. I agreed to let him go, but he wants to serve me. So I disabled some of our connection, but he still feels my anger and pain. Tanya follows close behind him, and that's when I see her lips are pink, as if she has been kissing someone. When I glance back at Melvon, he looks away with guilt etched all over his face.

"Tanya," I say, my voice low, but she knows.

Her eyes skirt to Melvon.

"I told her not to kiss me, but she insisted," Melvon says in a hurry.

Tanya strides up to him and slaps him across the face. Hard. He doesn't even flinch, but I know it hurts her because she shakes out her hand.

"You kissed me back, vampire."

"After you stuck your tongue down my throat," he calmly says back to her. She goes to hit him again, but he grips her wrist, preventing her from doing so.

"It's best you keep your hands to yourself, witch," he bites back.

She pulls her hand free and turns to face me. "What's going on?" Her arms cross over her chest.

She has grown up a little. But she is still the more timid and quiet of us all. I don't like what is happening between her and Melvon, but I'm not going to get involved. That's between them.

"Viper sent our sister through a portal," I inform her. Her eyes go wide, and she looks at John, then back to me.

"What? How?"

I shrug. "Bronik informed me."

"And what is he doing to get her back?" she asks.

"He left. I don't think he's doing anything."

"Who else can create a portal?" Tanya asks.

"Only Viper. The queen could, too, but she's dead." I watch as her shoulders droop in disappointment. I feel it as well.

"What about Death? He wouldn't let her die," Tanya says, hopeful.

"I don't even know if he can see that far. He is death to our world, but the other one? We know nothing but stories told to make us fear it."

"Should we call him?" Tanya offers. "Talia calls him when she's really angry at him."

"And he doesn't come," I remind her.

"Apart from that one time." We both stay silent for a moment. Then, in unison, we start screaming for him. Of course, nothing happens, and we both look like fools screaming at the night sky. When our voices grow hoarse, I glance over at Tanya.

"We could try to kill ourselves, but you know... not succeed."

"Fucking hell. No," John utters, shaking his head.

Her idea isn't all that bad. But it's a risk we aren't sure about. Would he even come, then?

"Halaba girls, you are mighty noisy." Everyone swings their heads around to find Death, or Grim, as Talia calls him, standing behind us. "Your sister?" he asks, checking around.

"Not here," Melvon answers.

"Where is she?" He focuses on me.

"She went through a portal," I tell him.

He doesn't look shocked, just worried. His brows crease together, and he pulls his lips in tightly.

"Can you get her back?" I ask him.

"No. Other worlds are not our responsibility. We have never been able to go to any others."

"Will she survive? What do you know of it?"

"I know a lot of things, but only from those who have told me. I hear of a beautiful world where flowers blossom in all types of different colors. A world that is so physically remarkable, but also filled with great danger. What we know is that yorks possess the other world. One slipped through a portal once and took half our population many years ago. How the other world has managed to stay alive is beyond me. The only thing we Angels can think of is that they have someone very powerful protecting them." He pauses, and his tone has me weary. "Do not call for me again."

Before he goes, I reach for him. He glances at my

51

hand on his arm and then back to me. His eyes, a deep silver, stare into mine. If I knew better, I would drop his arm and run. No one should be touching Death. Yet Talia does it with ease.

"Will she survive?" I ask. "How do I find a portal?"

"If you go through a portal, you will be sure to die. You are weak, Tatiana, compared to your sister. You *will* die." And then he is gone.

John comes up behind me and touches my back, rubbing small circles to keep me grounded.

"Valefar!" I scream. "Valefar!"

"No, Tatiana. No," John says, but it's too late. Valefar appears in front of me. I offer him my hand, and we are gone before anyone can say anything.

"Your mate is going to kill me," Valefar says as we materialize in front of the castle doors. They open to reveal Viper standing on the other side. His eyes flick to Valefar, then to me.

"I cannot open it," is all he says, knowing full well why I am here.

"Lies. You did it before, do it again." Viper's eyes lock on Valefar.

"Tell her."

"He is telling the truth. He did it last time with a potion that was made for the queen. He used it on your sister to open the portal."

I swing my head around. "Make me the potion," I demand.

"The price you must pay is death, little one. Do you understand? Death of someone you love greatly. Veronica was happy to sacrifice those she loved for power. Are you willing to do the same?" he asks.

"Whose death?" I ask him on a whisper.

"John's," he replies.

I offer Valefar my hand. "Take me back."

When we reappear, I find John in wolf form, destroying everything around him. Valefar is quick to disappear, and I walk over to John. He spots me straight away and comes running to me. He doesn't change—he stays as a wolf. His head rubs on my belly, smelling me before he finally does change.

"What's wrong?" he asks, the love he has for me seeping into my very soul.

It's then I realize that I would sacrifice my sister for this man.

"We need to hope with everything we have she finds her way back," I tell him with teary eyes.

"She will. She is your sister, after all." He kisses me and whispers words of protection. And I know for the next century, I won't be leaving his sight.

Chapter Six

TALIA

It's been a week, and I'm still here. I've tried everything I can think of to open a portal, but I just can't do it. Not even a flicker or a glimmer of something. Anything.

Everywhere I go, I have a guard with me: One, in particular, is quite nice. He talks to me more than the others do. He is interested in where I come from, and I ask him to take me to the village where others who have fallen from the portal are located. He nods and tells me he will ask for permission.

Permission?

I didn't realize I was a prisoner.

The following day, I decide I will simply sneak out, but the guard is at my door when I wake.

"I can accompany you today to the village."

"Your king allowed this?" I ask, and he nods.

"You'll need a coat... it's cold outside of the castle." I open the cupboard, which is now stocked full of clothes, none of which I requested, but I'm thankful for all the same. I slip on a pair of sneakers and grab a coat before I follow the guard out the door. He leads the way until we reach the main entrance. The gate is like an old boom gate that drops down over a moat. Guards stare at us, but none of them say a word as I fall into step next to him.

"Thank you for this," I say to him.

The guard gives me a nod. He seems to be confused for a moment, then shakes his head and faces forward again.

"Do you have family here?" I ask.

"Yes, I have a partner and two kids."

I smile up at him. "And do you live in the castle?"

"No, only you and the king do."

I'm taken aback by this knowledge. "Not even Levy?" I inquire.

"No, she lives with the rest of us."

I didn't expect that answer. I assumed she lived in the castle since she seems to know her way around everywhere, and the king even instructed her on what to do with me. I'm not really sure about their relationship, and I try not to care. But I'm not going to lie— the king is intriguing.

"Does everyone who falls from the portal stay at the castle?" I question.

"No, you are the first."

"Is that... weird?" My eyebrows draw together in concern.

"Yes." He pulls his jacket tighter and does up the buttons as we move farther away from the castle. We walk quietly for a good hour, and I can tell he is comfortable with the silence. I guess as a guard, it may be what he's used to. Me, not so much. I miss my sisters and the loud noises they make and even just their laughter.

"Why is it colder here?" I finally ask between chattering teeth.

"The yates aren't too far from where we are now. So far, we have a barrier keeping them out, and it seems to be working, but the cold is not something we can stop."

"How many people live in the village?"

"About two hundred."

That's when I see it up ahead. Small little houses are nestled together in a circle, with a playground and other essentials centered in the middle. It's like their own barrier of houses. Every house is brown, with not one standing out more than the other. When we reach the first house, a little girl with blonde hair comes running toward us. The guard drops to a crouch, picks her up, and then swings her around. She giggles as he kisses her cheek before they both look at me.

"This is Talia," the guard says.

I feel bad I haven't learned his name.

I offer her my hand.

"It's a pleasure to meet someone so pretty. And what is your name?" The guard smiles at me as he looks at his daughter. I can see the resemblance, as it's more than obvious.

"Amirka," she says. And then her head falls onto her father's shoulders.

"I'm sorry, I never asked your name," I say to the guard.

"Adam," he tells me.

Another little girl runs over, followed closely by a lady with blonde hair. She walks over, kisses Adam on the lips, and falls into his side as if she belongs there as she glances at me with ease.

"Hi. We have heard so much about you."

"All good, I hope." I smile.

"Of course. Adam thinks you are fantastic. Come, meet some of the others."

I follow her into the middle area, where people seem to be gathering. Some offer me small smiles while others get up and leave.

"Don't worry about them. Our numbers are slowly dwindling, and everyone is worried about what that could mean for us," she explains in a small voice. "We used to be a large village..." She looks around. "There were thousands of us. Now we are all that's left."

"You!" I hear thrown my way and turn to find Levy standing at a door. "You are not welcome here."

"King Maxilliam instructed I bring her," Adam says.

"Well, you can take her right back to where you found her." Levy crosses her arms over her chest.

"How come she isn't dead yet?" I ask Adam, to which his wife tries to hide her laugh.

"Because unlike *you*, I know my place, *witch*."

"Witch. You say it as if it's a bad word spilling off your tongue when it's who I am. You need to try harder."

"Witch?" someone asks as they step closer.

"Oh, Ron... you are from her world."

I look over to see a man standing not too far from where we are. He has a mustache and is overly large, his big belly hanging over his pants as he stares at me.

"Why don't you teach this *witch* the ways of our world and how to better handle herself." Levy flicks her hair, turns with a scoff, and walks away.

"She doesn't like you all that much," Adam's wife comments. "But from what I hear, she has good reason not to."

"And what did you hear?"

"You are staying with the king. It's where she wants to be. It's everything she has worked toward, and you come along and get a room that was meant to be hers."

"My room is hers?" I ask, shocked.

No wonder she's angry at me.

"No, technically, it never was. She just thinks it is and that she deserves it. King Maxilliam has been entertaining her because he knows that we are growing weaker, and the only way to grow stronger is to keep our population growing. And King Maxilliam is the strongest of us all, but he is fair. And to be honest, he doesn't love her, even though it's obvious she loves him," Adam replies.

"I feel bad for her. She has turned down every last person while waiting for him," Adam's wife adds.

I glance at Ron, who has been watching me. "Why did the queen send you through the portal?" he asks me.

"It wasn't the queen. It was Viper."

He stares at me, wide-eyed, rubs his jaw, and looks to the ground.

"Viper?" he asks.

"Yes."

"And the queen?"

"Dead," I reply.

His eyes go big at this news.

"Dead. Oh my God, who did it?"

"Me," I reply without hesitation.

"You? How could you defeat her? She was mighty powerful. The only person I have seen more powerful than her is King Maxilliam." He squints his eyes, recognition flaring behind his gaze. "I know who you are now. You're one of the Halaba girls."

"Yes..." I pause. "And are you a wolf?" I ask, not wanting to assume. For all I know, he could be a human.

"I am. The queen didn't approve of me crossing the border, so she threw me down without warning, and poof, I ended up here." He waves his hands around.

"Are there any seers left?" I ask.

"A few. The yorks have killed most." He scratches his chin again. "None have warned us of your appearance, though. And they usually know when someone arrives." I say nothing to his words. "Is John still alive?"

"He is, and found his mate as well."

Ron smiles widely, his white teeth shining. "Who?"

"My sister." His smile drops.

"A wolf and a witch." His head shakes. "That's not common... or even heard of."

"Does it matter who you are here? Does power

60

matter within couples?" I ask, genuinely interested in how things work in this world.

Adam and his wife have walked off with their children, and Ron escorts me to the center of the circle, where a large bench sits. The area is quite peaceful, with the sun starting to set as we sit.

"Here, it's different. To those of us in the village, it doesn't matter, but for the king, it does. Levy is strong... her power is incredible. But she holds no other greater power. Some say he is settling. But settling for someone who loves you, is that really what he wants?"

I sit back in my seat and look at the sky.

"Is the king a good ruler? At least better than Queen Veronica?" The pink flowers hanging off the trees sway in the gentle breeze as I look up to the sky.

"Yes, he cares for his people, and he is just with punishments. I would choose to live here a thousand lives over than back there with her."

"But your world here is dying," I say, turning back to him.

He nods past the house. "If you step farther out past the houses, you will hear them. But bear in mind, whatever they say is fake. Once you reach a pole that is flashing bright yellow, don't go any farther. Anything on this side is real, but anything on that side is fake and only wants one thing."

"What's that?"

He sucks in a breath before he says the words, "To kill and consume you."

I stand and stride in that direction. No one stops me or tells me not to go. Once I pass the last house, it becomes dark. I continue until I get to the yellow light, then I stop in my step, not daring to go any farther, as instructed.

"Witch. Witch. Witch. Why don't you come say hello? We have something sweet for you." Peering into the darkness, there's a face I hate, one I would cross this path to destroy.

Veronica.

Oh, how I despise her with every fiber of my being.

"Do you not wish to know my secrets, witch? Of how to open a portal?" it asks. "Come on, witch... you know you want to know."

"If you tell me the spell, I'll consider it." I smile.

Fake Veronica sneers through her teeth at me. "Now, where would be the fun in that? You would leave straight away, and our end of the deal we would not receive."

"Talia." I turn to find King Maxilliam standing next to me.

"Where did you come from?" I ask, stepping back. "You aren't one of them, are you?" I question while pointing to the black shadows. The whole thing is weird. It's like a black bubble until it's a person, and when you look at that person, you would think it's real. They're exactly who they look like to a T, including how they sound and every subtle mannerism. The resemblance to the person they impersonate is perfectly done.

"I am not. But why are you so close to the border?"

"Our king, our king. Oh, what a wonderful king you are," one sings.

When I turn to its voice, I see it's a small woman. Her hair is white, and she has bright red lips and a sweet smile. Maxilliam's jaw tightens before he turns to me.

"Who is that to you?" I ask him.

"Before they consumed this world, I thought I was in love. Her name was Penelope." When I glance back, the white-haired girl is blowing kisses to Maxilliam.

"You thought?" I ask, frowning when I see the look on his face.

"Talia." My head swings around to the sound of that voice. Grim stands in the dark shadows, dressed in all black, his silver eyes shining back at me. I go to step forward, but a hand grips my arm and pulls me back.

"Who is that to you?" he asks with concern.

"That is Death," I whisper.

Chapter Seven

"D eath?" he questions, his concern morphing into confusion.

I look away from those silver eyes and into sky-blue ones. The king's eyes seem to have changed to a deeper color in this light. How different are Death and Maxilliam?

"Why am I staying in your castle?"

"Because he wants to see what's under that dress," the white-haired girl replies.

"You are there because it's the safest place to be," Maxilliam corrects.

"But most of your travelers are sent out here, are they not?"

"Yes, they are."

"Yet, I am not."

"No, you are not."

64

"Again, why?"

He turns his focus to the light, the one that indicates where we need to stop. "Because you are different. I knew it from the moment I saw you."

"I want you to know something. I'm in love with someone else." He stands there, unmoving as he stares at me, not saying anything, until his eyes shift back to the shadows.

"Death," he states.

"Yes," I reply, nodding my head.

"Sometimes love can be tricky. This Death you are in love with, does he feel the same way?" I turn and look back at the shadow as well. His dark hair is tied back, silver gaze firmly on me—what I wouldn't give to touch him.

"I think he does, but it's complicated." I give a shrug.

"All the best loves are," he utters. "Can I see your power?" he asks. "Peachies are interested in you, and I would like to know what type of power you hold. To my knowledge, most witches hold the power of a single element."

"I hold all," I tell him.

"I would still like to know. Can you show me?"

I bite my bottom lip before answering, "I can borrow power by touching someone."

"Borrow?" he asks, lifting a brow.

"Yes," I say as I step closer to him. I lift my hand but don't reach for him. He glances at me curiously. "Can I touch you?"

"Yes, you may." With his permission, I lift my hand and lay it on his arm. The minute I find his bare skin, I feel the buzz coming from him.

What *power*.

What absolute breathtaking power he holds.

I feel myself siphoning before I can stop myself. I know my eyes are changing color because the shock on his face tells me as he stares at me in awe. I manage to tear my hand away, and then I fall to the ground from the effort. Maxilliam reaches to help me to stand, but I pull him down with me.

"You are strong," I whisper as I mold myself to him. The high from his power is heady, overwhelming my senses. "I can feel what you feel. How beautiful is that?" I press my head into his chest, and he gently strokes my hair.

"Are you okay?"

I look up at him through my lashes and smile. "You are really pretty. Did you know that? All that chiseled jaw and eyes as blue as the sky. I bet you get a lot of female attention."

"Not from those I want it from."

His name is called, but neither of us pays any attention. We can't seem to stop staring at each other, our eyes roving over each other's faces in uninhibited fascination.

"Can I kiss you?" he asks on a low breath. I feel the question flowing through me before I answer with little thought.

I offer him a small smile and simply nod before he leans down, and his lips dance across mine. He tastes of apples and something a little darker, an edge that has me instantly craving more. His tongue slides across my lips before I open my mouth and let it move between mine with a delicately dominant stroke. He kisses me with a force I can't comprehend, or maybe I'm just too high to fully work it out. One thing I know is that this kiss rivals Death's kiss, which pains me a little.

Reaching up, I touch his shoulder, slide my hand to the nape of his neck, and give him back his power. When I feel it has all slithered away, I break the kiss, turning my head to the side as I lie still in his lap. When I open my eyes, I see Levy standing there with half the village watching us.

Her eyes flicker between colors, but I choose not to think about it too much and glance back to Maxilliam. "Your people are here."

With a snap of his fingers, I feel us move. We are no longer sitting on the ground in the dirt but lying on a bed—my bed, to be precise. When I realize where we are, I sit straight up. Maxilliam remains in his reclined position, watching me.

"Max—" I stop partway through saying his name.

"You can call me that from now on. Max. I like the way it sounds from your lips."

I stand and start pacing back and forth. "Your power," I say, shaking my head. "I've felt power like yours before. But not all at once." I stare at him in disbelief. "What are you?"

He smirks. "Part Angel, part demon."

"How…" I start, my mouth not even forming the words I want to speak. "That doesn't make sense."

"Neither do you, but here you stand."

"Yes, here I stand," I agree, pausing in my steps.

"Do you know what you are?" he asks, his eyes searching mine.

"I am a witch."

"You are, but you are also more. Do you know what else?"

I look at him, baffled and frustrated. My hands grip my dress, not having thought I could be different from my sisters. How is that possible? We are all the same. We appear the same, were born the same day different years, yet the possibility—

"Would you like me to guess?" he interrupts my raging thoughts by pulling my attention back to him, where he is now sitting on the edge of the bed.

"Sure, but I know who my father and mother were. My sisters and I all look alike.

"That doesn't mean one of you can't have a different father."

"My mother would have told me," I say. But as the words leave my lips, I'm not so sure.

"Not necessarily." He shakes his head. "How would you tell your child that they are the outcome of someone you didn't want them to know existed?"

"Existed?" I ask, confusion raging through me.

"Yes. I believe you are part demon. But not just any demon. The King of Hell himself..." He pauses, but continues when I don't react. "Only he had your power. I've not known nor heard of any other being having that kind of power." I walk over and sit on the bed with him, my mind spinning from this revelation. "Have you asked a seer, perhaps?"

A laugh tickles my throat.

"No, the one seer I know hates me."

"Give me your hand." I hold it out to him, and before I know it, we are back at the border with the bright, flashing yellow light. All eyes turn to us, and Levy runs straight to Max, her hands going around his neck. She hugs him to her, and he stands there stiffly, not reciprocating any of the attention she is showing him.

I glance at the crowd and see Ron, with Adam still in his uniform, standing next to him, looking at me.

"Levy." Max says her name, and she pulls away from him, wiping at her tears and staring at the ground. I feel bad for her, I do. He doesn't want her the way she wants him, which must be heartbreaking. His eyes find mine, and I hold them for a moment before I look away.

"I was worried she hurt you." Levy tries to touch him, but he holds out his hand to stop her.

"Maxilliam." The shadows are back, calling him, but he pays them no attention.

"Did she hurt you?" Levy pushes.

"No, she did not."

"But we saw she had you under a spell," she says, not realizing that she should probably stop questioning her king.

Max looks at her dead in the eye. "She did *not* spell me," he says again. "But I believe she can open a portal to her world to get us all through." Shock at his statement ripples through everyone, including me.

"A portal? Me?" I question, my spine straightening with a shiver.

Maxilliam steps around Levy and comes straight toward me. He captures my hand, giving it a squeeze. "You. You have the power, but you aren't quite strong enough, whereas I am. I can give you the right amount of power to do it." Everyone goes quiet. Not one word is uttered. "Talia, I can give you the power. You felt it, correct?"

"I did."

The king turns away from me and searches the crowd with his eyes. "Alan."

A man steps forward, and I know straight away he is a seer as he has the same eyes as Viper.

"Alan, would you help me with Talia?"

He bows. "Of course, sir."

Max starts walking away, guiding me along with him, and the villagers follow us, even Levy, who is glaring at me as if I am bacteria that grows on her feet. I probably am, but I'm going to take any chance I can get to return back to my family.

"We don't need her help," Levy yells as we enter the village, eyes on us the whole way.

Max stops and looks back to Levy, but chooses not to answer her before he points to the bench where Ron and I were sitting earlier.

"It takes a lot from you," he states, and I nod my head. "But you also get very high on it." I hide my smile, remembering that kiss. *Would I have kissed him if I hadn't taken his powers?*

"Alan, can you read her?"

Alan steps from the crowd and walks over to me.

71

He bends down until we are eye-to-eye and shakes his head. "I've never had this problem..."

"It's because she is stronger than you. She is blocking you."

I hear a loud gasp.

"But, my king, I can read you."

"Her power is stronger, she just doesn't have full access to it all yet." Everything and everyone seem to still. "Alan, you have seen and heard the spell for the portal. Once I give her my power, you can guide her. I need you to guide her, Alan. She will be stronger, but she is also on a high. You have the ability to manage a high, so I need it managed."

"You want to do it now?" I ask Max.

He simply nods.

I hear footsteps and see all the guards are now here. Glancing around, I take a deep breath. *What if I fuck this up and kill everyone?*

"You won't kill anyone," Max says, as if reading my mind.

"Max, I don't know..." I shake my head. Someone grunts at the sound of my words, but neither of us pays any attention.

"You let her call you that? You just stand there and let her call you Max?" Levy shrieks.

"Levy, now is not the time," Max replies.

She throws her hands up in the air. "I think now *is*

the time. You have everyone who lives here in this village in attendance. We should vote. We should get a say in this. Our opinion matters too."

Max stands, and he seems taller than almost everyone here. Actually, maybe he is.

"You wish to disobey me?" he asks darkly. And it's then I see a different side of him. He is usually calm and relaxed. But now, his back is straight, form intimidating, and his jaw is set in a hard line. His hands clench at his sides.

When I look past him to Levy, I watch as she changes. She doesn't change into just anyone, though. No, she picks me. The crowd gasps as she starts to speak. "Is this what you want? I can be *this* for you, King Maxilliam. Or do you prefer Max now?"

"Levy, I've let enough slide. You *will* change back right now and get rid of this thing you have going on."

"It was me you were meant to choose. Why do you let this abomination get away with so much?"

"Levy, change and stop! Now!" I feel her eyes shift to me. They lock on as she stalks past Max and straight in my direction. She gets close and drops down, so we are eye-to-eye.

"You can't have him. He was never yours. Everything was perfect until you came along."

"Was it, though? Has he kissed you, Levy?" I taunt, because I can't help myself. I watch as my mouth on

73

her face turns into a sneer. *Ewww, do I look like that when I'm angry?*

"Die, witch!" She transforms back into herself and pulls a knife from her pants, raising it above me. I manage to catch it mid-air while my other hand comes up and lands on her bare shoulder. I start taking power from her, and her eyes go wide as she drops the knife. Then I feel her weaken, so I release her and step back. She falls to the ground, landing like a piece of shit.

"Talia." I turn to see Max, and I smile up at him.

"She has some juice, but not quite like yours."

"You allow this?" Levy gasps, hardly able to move from the ground. "You let her harm your people."

"You attempted to kill her, Levy. We all saw it," Adam says.

Max looks at him and nods. "Please remove Levy and hold her back while we work." He shifts his attention to where she's slumped on the ground. "You are coming with us, no matter how mad I am at you right now. Even though you defy me, I will not leave you here."

"You should," Levy says.

I start to laugh, and Max steps forward, his hand resting on my hip to steady me. "Your eyes. Why do they do that?" he questions, his gaze searing.

"Who knows." I find myself leaning into him,

74

resting my head on his shoulder. "Are they pretty, though?"

"Yes," he replies in a low voice that only I can hear. I smile into his chest as I feel Alan approach.

"It is time, miss."

I offer Alan my hand, and he takes it, helping me back to the bench. Alan leans in and says, "I've seen you before, miss. You truly are remarkable."

"You've seen me?" I ask.

"Yes, when you were born. All us seers had a vision of you. Of what you would become."

I didn't know this. How could nobody have told me this before now?

"I'm sorry you got sent here," I reply.

"I'm not, miss. It has been an honor knowing you all." He bows his head. "May I touch you?" I nod, and he places his hands on my head. It's soothing, and I close my eyes for a brief second before I open them to smile up at him. "That was calming."

"Thank you." He removes his hands, and I look at Max.

"Are you ready?" he asks, stepping closer.

"I think you should sit on the ground. What if you fall when I take your power?"

"I appreciate your concern, but I am stronger than you think."

"I can taste how strong you are, Max." I grin up at

him. "At least sit next to me." He does, and I reach for his hand. "What if I try to kiss you again?" I ask him in a small voice.

"What a delight that would be."

I can't help the warmth that floods me at his words.

Chapter Eight

As I touch him, he offers me one of those smiles that have started to make my stomach flutter.

"Are you sure?" I place my hands on his shoulders.

"Positive," he states.

I close my eyes and immediately begin to feel the pull of his power as it slithers into me. Max's power is unlike any other I have felt. It holds something I'm not quite sure how to describe, like a feeling of home, I guess. It's comforting, in every way possible, and it's as if his power was meant to be shared with me.

I pull away and open my eyes. Max is watching me with an eager expression, not sure what is happening.

"You are so beautiful." I cup his cheek.

Maxilliam lets my touch linger for a moment before he looks past me to Alan. "Do it."

When Alan lays his palm on me, a relief washes over me yet again. I feel myself drain from the high, but not as if I am coming down and need to sleep. It's more of an alertness, a sharpening of my senses.

"Miss, I'm to whisper the words to you, and you will need to say them loud enough for the gods to hear."

I look at him, confused. *Gods?* No one uses that term anymore. Where I am from, Gods don't exist, just the one who sent the Angels.

Nodding, I glance back to Max. He stands and drops my hands, then backs away. He starts pushing everyone back, so it's just Alan and me now with a large space around us.

Then Alan quietly recites the words I am to say.

"*Worlds apart.*
Worlds collide.
Give me worlds to combine."

I repeat his words aloud, and I feel something being sucked from me when I do. When Alan lifts his hands, the high comes right back, but I feel it being pulled from me in an instant, like a snake releasing its hold and slithering away to something else.

When I finally get my wits about me and manage to glance down, I see a portal. Max pushes his people through as soon as it is wide enough. I'm unable to move, as it takes all of Max's power from me. I drop down to all fours when I feel it start to touch my own power. As soon as I do, Max is there, lifting and throwing me over his shoulder.

"As soon as you are through, it will close."

I feel him moving, but I'm too drained. It's a similar sensation to when I give someone their power back. Exhausting. Almost debilitating. However, this time is worse. This time it's my power.

"Hold on, Talia."

Goddamnit! I can't do what he is saying, but I feel the pull when he leaps into the opening, and then a drop. Maxilliam holds me to him as we fall, as if he can protect me.

Maybe he can.

I have no idea.

My eyes become heavy, and soon everything stops moving.

"Talia, can you hear me?" Someone caresses my face. I manage to open my eyes. "Talia, take what you need." I feel something warm and smooth under my palms. When I look at them, I see they are under Max's shirt, resting against his bare skin. "Talia." He basically growls my name. "Take."

And I do.

I pull as little as I can because it's hard to do so. I feel it right away, and when I've gotten enough, I stop and drop my head back.

"Where are we?"

"Is this your world?" Max asks, angling my head so I can see where we are. He lifts me up again, and this time he carries me gently instead of putting me over his shoulder.

"Alan?" I ask.

"It took a lot out of Alan. He has passed out." Tearing my gaze away from those icy-blue eyes, I check my surroundings.

My eyes widen when I see a familiar house. "Stop," I say, and he does. "That's where I lived." I smile, point in its direction. Half the house is still missing from attacks, and I haven't been back since. It appears so ruined, devastating, so vacant.

"Should we be worried about the witches?" Maxilliam asks me. I see a few forms step out and look our way. Some lock eyes with me and go straight back to where they came from.

"Talia."

Everyone stops at the voice.

Standing in front of us is Bronik, who I once thought was incredibly handsome, but now I can't stand the sight of him.

"Angel," Max hisses.

Bronik turns to Max, who is still holding me.

"Half-breed," Bronik growls.

"You can put me down now," I tell Max. As I get my feet under me, I see him.

Everything stops.

Everything falls away.

Apart from him and me.

"Little fighter," he whispers, and I feel the hairs on my neck rise as I stare at him.

Max is still as I try to get out of his hold and turn around. When I'm finally free, my heart picks up a beat, and my hands grow sweaty at the sight of him.

"I thought you weren't visiting me again." Death glances behind me, and his jaw tightens, then he starts grinding his teeth as he glares at Max.

"Sometimes you have to break the rules." His voice is dark, and if I didn't know better, I would say he's angry.

"Do you know who my father is?" I ask.

Death's silver eyes leave Max to lock on to me.

"Yes."

"You never told me?" I ask shocked.

"No, I didn't."

"Why?" My voice raises a little as he looks at me.

"You had to find out for yourself." I clench my jaw, and when I go to move closer to him, I almost fall.

He catches me, leans to my ear, and whispers, "I can smell him all over you."

"And whose fault is that?" I bite out, pushing away from him.

"What do you mean?"

"You didn't want me, and sometimes a girl wants to be wanted," I tell him as I take a seat on the ground. I lift some dirt and run it through my hands. "I don't think you should come back again."

"Okay," he replies, and I hate that his agreeance makes my chest ache.

"You told me once when it came to my end, you saw who I was with, and it wasn't you. Who was it?" I ask, but it comes out more as a plea.

He stands there and just watches me. It feels like ages go by before he finally moves, and when he does, he looks at Max. His forehead pinches together, and then he is gone.

"Asshole!" I yell.

"Sorry?" I turn back to Max, who is looking at his hands and then at me, confused. "How did you get..."

He shakes his head and opens and closes his eyes a few times, trying to clear his mind.

Bronik smiles.

"Didn't take him long to find you."

Max and I both glance over at Bronik.

"Who?" Max asks.

"Her lover, of course. Death," Bronik replies.

Max's eyes find mine, and he holds them. I told him I was with someone else. And I can see him putting it all together as he stares at me, assessing the clear emotion written all over my face.

"Your sister is waiting for you with the wolves," Bronik adds before he disappears.

I look back at everyone else with us and spot Levy hiding among the crowd. She isn't sure about being here.

"I need to go to my sisters. It is safer where the wolves are," I tell Max. All his people look to him for guidance. "Vampires hold land not far from here, and they are known to provoke." Though the witches have made their own barriers and wardens to keep them out, some still manage to get through, from what I have heard.

"Lead the way," Max says, holding out his hand.

I nod and start walking, feeling the eyes on me from the town as we leave.

"Talia." Someone calls my name, but I keep up my steps. "Talia."

Eventually, I stop to see our old neighbor come out of her house.

"Francis," I say, turning as she makes her way over to us. Francis was one of my mother's friends and always chose to stay out of trouble. Never offering help in any way.

"Your mother gave me this, and now it's time I give it to you." She holds out a small diary, and I take the offering. Studying it, I'm confused as to what it might be.

"My sister gave this to Valefar," I say, amazed.

"She gave him a fake copy. This is the real one. She knew that one day someone would try to use it against you. So I have kept it hidden."

When I open the first page, I see my name written in my mother's handwriting. I glance up at Francis. "Thank you."

She nods before walking away.

"Your mother never told you much about who you were?" Max asks, coming to stand next to me. I start moving forward again, as does he, and everyone else follows.

"No, she didn't really get much of a chance." I wipe away a tear that runs down my cheek and hug the diary to my chest.

"And Death?" he inquires.

I side-eye him. He's dressed in his black outfit that molds to every perfect inch of his body. *I know what it feels like to touch that body.* I quickly look away.

"As I said, it's complicated."

"I have heard stories of Death from your world. Not much is known about him, but what is... is that no one sees him." He pauses, shaking his head. "Yet, you do?"

"I do." I tell no lies because it's simply not worth it. It's not anything new to me to hear someone ask why I see him.

I've always been able to see him. It's just how we have always been. Granted, he chooses when.

"It's not too much farther," I tell Max and pick up the pace. He matches my speed, and we walk in silence for what feels like forever while I clutch the diary to my chest the whole way.

I want to sit down and open it, then read it from front to back.

But I also desperately want to see my sisters.

I've missed them, and I can't imagine the turmoil I've caused Tatiana. She would have tried everything to get to me. That's just who she is, and I love her for it.

She will be an amazing mother, of that, I am sure.

And John? The way he loves her, their child is sure to have the same type of love.

"Miss." I turn around to find Alan behind me. I step to the side, and Max keeps on walking, with everyone following him.

"Alan, is everything okay?" I lift my hand toward him, but he pulls away and shakes his head.

"It's changed. Everything has changed," he says, looking around. "I had a son. I hid him before I was thrown through the portal."

"A son?" I ask, surprised.

He nods his head. "I can see him now that I am here. I hate to do this to you, but I have to leave."

"Why aren't you telling Max?"

He glances over to Max and then back to me. His white eyes hold mine. "It is not him who is destined to rule this world," he says, and I offer him a smile. "Thank you for bringing me back. I would never have imagined I'd be here again. I must go. I know my way to him. I can see him."

"Thank you, Alan," I reply, smiling.

He bows.

"No, thank you, my queen."

I don't bother correcting him.

When I can no longer see him, I turn to catch up with the group, but before I make it a few steps, I'm pushed to the ground. The diary falls out of my hand, and I turn to try to get it, crawling toward it, but a foot steps heavily on my hand. I hear the bones crunch and pull it straight back to me.

When I glance up, I see Levy standing there with an evil grin on her face before she strides away.

Hopefully, I won't kill her today.

But the possibility is there.

Chapter Nine

The wolves' land is ahead. When I reach the front of the line, there are two wolves snarling at Max from either side, but he doesn't seem fazed. I guess he wouldn't be, considering how strong he is.

I wonder how many people he could take down on his own.

I also wonder the same about myself.

As I push through to the front, one of the wolves stops snarling and shifts back to human form.

"You were gone," she states. "I was worried."

I remember this wolf, but I don't know her name. She's one of the few who isn't rude to me.

"I'm back. Are my sisters here?"

She nods and looks at the other wolf before it runs off.

"Bastian will get them. I don't think it's a good idea for everyone to enter... wolves are territorial." I nod in understanding. "Your sisters are going to be so happy to see you." I give her a soft smile as I check around. Everything seems to be pretty much the same except for some additional housing.

"Talia." I hear my name before I see her. When she comes into view, I rub my eyes. Am I seeing right? No, that can't be right. I've been gone less than two weeks. How is her stomach so large already? When she reaches me, she puts her arms around me, but I'm careful not to hug her too tightly because she has a large belly in the way. "I was so worried I would never see you again."

I pull back to find tears streaming down her face. With one hand resting on her shoulder, the other lowers to touch her belly. "How did you get so big?" I ask, rubbing her rounded stomach. Her gaze falls to the diary in my hand, and she reaches for it. I let her take it, and when she opens the cover, she starts reading the first page.

"How did you get this?"

"Francis held it for Mother. She said it was time to give it to me."

John comes over and gives me a one-armed cuddle. He gives the crowd of villagers a curious glance as he lets me go. "It's good to have you back."

I smile and look back at my sister.

"How did you get so big? I've only been gone a short time?" I ask again, and she frowns.

She reaches out and grasps my hand. "You've been gone for two years, Talia."

What? I'm glad I'm not holding anything because I would have dropped it instantly if I were.

"That can't be right."

"Time must work differently on the other side of the portal," Max conveys as he comes up next to me. He stands close, and Tatiana doesn't miss his nearness. Her eyes zoom in on us, and she raises a brow in question but doesn't say anything.

"Do you want to meet your niece? She reminds me of you," Tatiana says before she rubs her belly. "John thinks he will get a boy next, but I'm saying a girl." She smiles softly. "I've missed you."

"I missed you as well."

"Who are these people?" John asks, eyeing Max.

I spin around to see everyone standing back, waiting.

"These are King Maxilliam's people from the other world. We managed to escape through a portal to get here."

"How? We tried everything to open a portal, and we couldn't make one. Not even Valefar could without a steep price."

"Talia made one," Max says.

"How?" John asks in an almost bark. "That's impossible."

"Talia is very gifted and strong."

"I know," Tatiana says, but I can see it's still not making sense to them.

Max nods. "I loaned her my power," he explains, making Tatiana's mouth hang open at his words.

Her eyes fall on me. "You know what that does to you." She shakes her head. "I'm glad it worked, even if it was risky."

"Is Tanya here?" I ask. "And do you have somewhere everyone can sleep?" I ask, looking at John. "We aren't sure what we are going to do yet, or where we will go—"

"We?" Tatiana interrupts. "You plan to leave and go where they go?" She points her finger behind me to Max's people.

"I know the wolves won't be comfortable having everyone here, but for now, I am asking that they stay, have some food, and regroup." I glance over at John, who simply nods and turns back to his wolves.

"We will make room."

"We?" Tatiana asks again.

"They don't know this land. I do. Not all of it, but they need to rebuild. This is all new to them."

"Viper will not be happy. You have to speak to the king first before you take over more land," Tatiana says.

"Viper is still king? *How*? Why?"

"He's made it better, Talia. I know he's an absolute dick for what he did to you, but he's contained the vampires, and the humans feel safer now."

"What price is he demanding for that?" I question, knowing there's a catch for everything he does.

"Does it matter? It's better than what it used to be."

"Is it?" I shake my head. "You still stay in your areas as if we aren't all put on this earth to share. He believes separation is best. Max had his own world, and everyone stayed together and they got along. That was a better world than what we have. The witches have barriers up, which we only got through because we landed there. If we had tried to walk into town, I'm not sure we could have."

"The witches have put up spells to keep Viper out so he can't access them. And in return, they get no food," my sister says in a low voice.

"That's our home, Tatiana. You know that's not fair."

She throws up her hands. "I know. John sneaks them what he can. But if Viper found out, he would execute us."

"If I don't execute him first myself."

"You tried going against him last time and look where it got you. If he put you through another portal, could you survive?"

"You said he doesn't have access to portals."

"He says he doesn't, but that doesn't mean he isn't lying."

"What price do you pay to live here?" I demand.

She glances at her stomach and rubs it in circles. "A lot has changed, Talia. We didn't have you any longer."

"The witches are finally making a stand." I remind her, locking eyes on her hand which is touching her stomach.

"That's because one of their own isn't on the throne. You know we are the most powerful. It's why Veronica held it for as long as she did."

"It sounds like excuses," I say as John steps forward.

"Let's get you all some food and a place to sleep."

Max nods and thanks him, then turns back to his people and motions for them to follow John. My sister and I stay where we are. Max is still lingering when the last villager falls in behind John.

"I can stay," he says, low enough for only me to hear.

"It's fine," I tell him, so he nods and leaves.

My sister has a sour look plastered on her face when I turn back to her. "What? Does he think I would hurt my own sister?" Tatiana says, crossing her arms over her chest.

"He's new here, Tatiana."

"You like him," she states. "You don't need to confirm the fact, I can see you do." She watches as the group makes their way toward the houses. Max looks back at us as I step up next to my sister. "He likes you, too. I can tell."

"I know," I reply. I'm surprised she noticed.

She glances at me. "I don't know him, but I'm sure he would be a better option than Death," she whispers.

"Grim and I—"

"Have you seen him?" she asks.

"Yes, as soon as I arrived, after Bronik showed up."

"That asshole. I swear, if I could, I would let my wolves eat him."

"*Your* wolves?" *That's a new development.*

"Yes. I'm the mate to the alpha, so they are mine as well." She rubs her belly. "And we are creating more life."

"It really is beautiful." I reach for her stomach and hold my hand there. "What did you name her?" I ask Tatiana.

"Tamika. I wanted to keep the Ts alive." She smiles. "John suggested your name, but that is your name, and I knew one day you would find your way back to me."

She reaches for me again and pulls me to her. I hug her harder this time and hold on.

"Tamika's powerful. Not like you, but she is strong as well," she says. "She hasn't shown any signs of being able to shift yet, but John said to give it time. He first shifted when he was two, and she's coming up to two, so we will see."

I pull back and see something of a blur heading straight for me. Arms wrap around my neck and grip on for dear life. Tanya smiles as she pulls back, not letting me go.

"I didn't believe it when they said it. You *are* here." I look behind her to see Melvon.

"Melvon, say hello," Tanya encourages him closer. "Melvon and I got married," she says, clapping her hands. Tatiana rolls her eyes. "I love him." Melvon steps up and touches Tanya's hip and pulls her back to him. She falls effortlessly to his side.

Before I can say another word, I'm picked up and moved. Max now stands in front of me, blocking me from seeing my sister.

"Vampire," he hisses.

Tanya pushes Melvon behind her, but he steps back out and bares his teeth.

"Max... Melvon is good." I tap his shoulder.

"You said they served the queen and are awful."

Did I say that?

"Melvon is different," I tell him and swing back to my sister. "Married?" I ask, shocked. My sister slides her hand into Melvon's and leans against him.

"Yes, it took a bit of convening, but here we are." Tatiana turns to Max. "Why are you so fast?"

"Why are you a witch?" he replies. "It is not what I know... it's who I am," he answers simply.

"You were a king in your world. You realize in this one you are not?" Tatiana pushes.

"I am still my people's king, and I will do anything to protect them."

"What if it meant protecting them against her?" She nods to me.

What did she just say? My mouth gapes, eyes wide.

"Are you saying Talia is dangerous?"

Tatiana smirks.

"You know what she is."

Max simply nods, and Tanya stares at the three of us in confusion.

"I do. I knew as soon as I met her."

"Are you the same?" she asks.

"No, I am different," Max answers, leaving it at that. "Walk with me?" he asks, offering me his arm before addressing my sisters. "I only ask for a moment of privacy, and I will return her to you."

My sisters nod and smile.

I place my arm under his, and we take a left, away

from everyone, until we reach a tree. I remember this place. It's where Patrick was once waiting for me to cross the border all that time ago.

I miss him.

So much.

"Why do you look sad?" Max asks, reaching for my face. When he makes contact with my skin, I feel it everywhere. "Someone like you shouldn't be so sad."

"Someone like me?"

"Yes... beautiful." I take his words in and want to hold them close. He gives me things that Grim does not. But I still feel something for Grim that's beyond my control.

I want to kiss him.

I want him to want me again.

"I lost someone, and this spot reminds me of them," I tell him. "Why did you want a moment with me?"

"So I can do this."

He leans down and doesn't give me a moment to think of anything else as his lips descend upon mine. They don't slam into me in unbridled passion. Instead, they are gentle and giving. He tastes me before I feel his tongue slide between my lips, tangling with mine in a languid exploration. I fist my hands in his shirt and pull myself to him, feeling his strength as he wraps an arm around my waist. When our bodies are flush, one of his hands skirts up my back, holding me to him at my nape. We dance with kisses as fire dances with water —it's exciting and new, and if you get too close, you may feel a burn, but what an intoxicating burn it would be.

When he pulls back, I feel his reluctance to let me go.

"I wanted to be able to kiss you without the high," he says, kissing my cheek before he walks off, leaving me standing alone under a tree.

It's not pink or purple like his world.

But it sure is beautiful.

Chapter Ten

It's late when I finally make my way back to the group. All of Max's people are surrounding a large fire. Some stand off in the distance while others eat whatever food they are supplied.

When I pass Max, I can feel his eyes on me, but I don't meet his gaze. I maintain my path to John's home.

Pushing the door open, I hear a girl squeal, followed by a loud cry.

"Tamika, come here." A little bundle runs toward me and then stops. She smiles up at me, and I bend down to her. "Hello." Her cheeks go red in the sweetest blush. Tamika's rosy cheeks remind me of Tatiana's.

"Oh, you are back. Good. Pick that evil child up and join me for dinner." I smile down at Tamika and

99

offer her my hands. She thinks about it and, before I can pull away thinking she doesn't want a stranger to pick her up, she jumps, and I just manage to catch her.

"You look just like your mama," I coo, smiling at her as we walk into the kitchen. She giggles and pulls my hair.

"Same color as ours," I tell Tatiana.

"She keeps me on my toes, that one." Tatiana's cooking on the stove and it makes my stomach grumble.

"That smells good," I comment, walking to the table and sitting down, still holding little Tamika in my arms.

"I'm cooking the best for you. Does your king want to join us?" She wiggles her brows. John walks in and heads straight to Tatiana, kissing her cheek before he squeezes her hip and turns to us. He strides over, and Tamika reaches for him.

"He seems like a good king. His people respect him," John says, and I can only nod. "Your lips are red." He smirks.

"You kissed him? Is that the first time?" Tatiana gasps, abandoning her food and walking over to me.

"No, I was high on power the first time."

"Wow, okay. So why did he kiss you, then?"

I touch my lips.

"He wanted me to know what it felt like without the power high."

"Okay, swoon. He definitely likes you. A lot." She sits opposite me and leans on the table. "I bet he's a good kisser. Was it good?"

I nod my head, my stomach still fluttering. "It was."

Tanya walks in, spots us, and sits down. John holds their daughter as he takes over the cooking while we all sit and catch up.

"So, the king has a thing for you. He's very protective, that's for sure," Tanya says, reaching for the bowl in the middle of the table, picking up a delicious red apple, then biting a chunk. "No more you and Death, then?" she asks. "Do you really just get over someone like him? I mean, your king is handsome and all, but Death?" She rolls her eyes and sits back, biting her apple.

Tanya was always known as the quiet one of the three of us, but it seems she has come out of her shell a little more. She was never quiet with us growing up, only with others, but I can see a change in her now. I think it's for the better, and I have a feeling it's all to do with what happened with Veronica. She may not want to appear weak or to be used again.

The thing is, Tanya isn't weak. Her powers just aren't as strong as mine and Tatiana's. But now she has

Melvon—a very weird coupling, I'm not going to lie—
and it seems to work.

"Tanya," I say, ignoring the question.

"Hmm..."

"Does Melvon feed from you?" I ask, wondering
where he would eat. Wolves and vampires don't really
mix well, so I'm surprised he's still here.

She blushes.

"He feeds from me." She pulls her top down to
reveal bite marks at the top of her breast. I'm sure my
face morphs into a *what the fuck* look because she
quickly hides it. "I enjoy it, and it's something both of
us agreed to. He didn't want to at first because he was
too afraid it would hurt me." She bites her lip. "It
doesn't... it makes me horny."

John coughs from the cooking area, and Tanya
blushes.

"What if he took too much? Vampires get
addicted."

"He doesn't. He's so careful, Talia. You don't
know him like I do. He's careful with me."

"But he is a vampire."

"I've had these conversations with her already,"
Tatiana says. "She is safe with him, believe it or not. He
protects her. And that's not from a spell, he just does
it. We weren't aware vampires could feel like we do.
But Melvon proves they can."

"He's good to me," she says again, and I reach for her hand.

"I'm glad." I give it a squeeze and pull back.

"Is Max good for you? Or Death?" Tanya asks. "I feel like you may have to work that out."

"I saw Grim. I told him not to come back again." Biting my lip, I lay my head on the table. "And Max... well, Max has his own issues he needs to deal with. Like a whole new world and a crazy, possessive girlfriend or wannabe girlfriend, I'm not really sure which," I add, shrugging my shoulders.

"I invited him in for dinner," John says, pulling my attention to him. "It's smart to be in good standing with someone new, and I can smell the power radiating from him." He pauses, then asks me, "What is he?"

I feel all eyes on me, waiting for an answer.

How do I tell them?

Should I tell them?

It's not my place, but they are my family, and I have never kept secrets before, apart from Grim. But that situation was different.

"He is part Angel and part demon," I announce.

"And I'm part demon," I say as I look at Tatiana. "You knew this already, didn't you?" She nods, and her eyes glance to the diary on the counter.

"The copy I had didn't say who your father was, just that you were part demon. The original diary might tell us more." She looks back at me. "Have you read it?

"No. Max has ideas, though."

"Really? Who?" Tatiana asks.

"He thinks it's the King of Hell."

The whole room goes silent at my words.

"I..." Tatiana shakes her head. "How do you feel about that?"

I shrug my shoulders.

"I haven't really had time to absorb it. I do hope what I read in that diary will tell me." I look over to it. "Why did she keep so many secrets from us?" I whisper.

"I don't know."

A knock sounds on the back door, and John goes to answer it.

"Angel and demon, ha. That's a big one," Tatiana muses, sitting back and rubbing her belly.

Max walks in. He greets us all, but his eyes hold on me a little longer.

"Dinner is ready. I'm glad you chose to join us."

"I cannot decline an invitation. That would be rude of me." He smiles, heads straight to where I am, and sits beside me.

Everyone notices but says nothing as the food is served.

* * *

We remain in this place between kisses and touches for the rest of the week. Max and John get along great. When I'm not sleeping, I am reading through my mother's diary, trying to work it all out.

I can't quite do it.

When I get sick of reading, I get up and walk outside, and that's where Max usually finds me.

He asks to speak to me, takes me to the tree, and kisses me.

We haven't gone any further, and I'm thankful he isn't rushing me and that he wants to take his time.

His people have all settled in nicely and are getting along with the wolves, though yesterday, we had an attack from a group of four vampires.

Viper knows I am here.

I knew it wouldn't be long until he did. And to be honest, he isn't my main priority right now. I'm too busy trying to work out who I am. I still don't know her yet. And I want to.

This diary is meant to help me. But it's only leaving me more confused.

Walking out into the night, I see him before he spots me. Tents have been set up all around the wolves' houses. Max always makes sure everyone is doing okay before he settles, and I smile when I see him sitting in a group of people.

"I hate you." I don't even need to look to know who's standing next to me. "I hate that you came along and took him." We're both facing Max, and I can see him watching us. "Why did you have to come and ruin everything?"

"Your world was dying, Levy."

"No, it wasn't. He would have saved us." She turns away from Max to me and gets right in my face. "I will make you pay for taking him. He was meant to be mine. I've heard stories of you. The wolves talk. You had a thing with Death. Why don't you go back to him and leave us be?"

"*Levy.*" Max says her name abruptly from a short distance away. She smiles at him before she offers him her hand, but he doesn't take it.

"Walk with me?" she asks sweetly, but he disregards her completely.

"I need to talk to Talia."

Levy huffs, then snarls at me before she stomps off. I watch her go and feel him come up behind me. "Let's go for a walk. You look like you want to tear someone's head off."

"Yeah, your girlfriend's," I taunt. He grips my hand in his and starts pulling me. "Did you fuck her?" I ask him. When he doesn't answer me, I tug my hand free. He stops and turns around to face me. "Did. You. Fuck. Her?"

"Yes."

"Have you fucked her since meeting me?"

"No, and not for her lack of trying." My arms cross over my chest. "It didn't feel right. Don't ask me why, it just didn't. I have a feeling part of that is why she blames you."

"Oh, she blames me for everything," I point out.

"She should be thankful." Max reaches for my hand again and starts walking again. We fall into step with each other, and when we reach the tree, he sits on the ground and tugs me down to him. I climb onto his lap, straddling him, and push a dark strand away from his face.

"My people and I need to move on." I nod. "Do you know what I mean, Talia?"

"From leaving your place, you need to move on," I say, my fingers tracing down his cheek to his jaw.

His hands grip my hips, and he shakes his head. "No, we need our own space. This isn't ours... we are invading. I want to rebuild, make my people feel welcome."

"You are welcome," I tell him. He pulls at my hips until I scoot farther into his lap, where I can feel him. Everywhere. I lock my eyes with his ice blues and wonder why he makes me flutter, why he feels so right.

"It's because we are both a little wrong."

"Huh?"

"You're wondering why you have this pull toward me, correct? I can see it when you think too hard. You get a pinch between your brows right here." His finger gently rubs the spot he's talking about, and my eyes shutter in response. "What I'm saying is neither of us are purebloods... we are a little of this and that. There are not many like us. Angels and demons weren't allowed to fuck out of their race, especially to reproduce, yet here we are."

"Here we are," I say as one of my hands clasps his. When I look into his eyes, I lean in and can't help myself. I press my lips against his, and something rushes through me. What, I don't know. But it feels good.

Max releases my hand and pulls me even closer. My lower body moves against him, and his hands begin to roam. He slides a hand up the back of my shirt and strokes my spine, his kisses never stopping. It's torture and pleasure all in one. Breaking our kiss, I smile down at him.

"I think this is my new favorite tree." He chuckles, and I can't help the laugh that bubbles out of me.

"Mine too." I reach for my shirt and pull it off over my head. His eyes never leave mine to wander my body, even though I am giving him permission to.

"I'm not sure you are ready for this kind of commitment," he says. "I've fucked before, Talia, but this, this will be anything but. I feel something for you that I have never felt for anyone." I lift his hand and put it over my breast, right above my heart.

"Can you feel it?" I ask.

"Your heart?" I nod. "I can."

"It's beating fast." He goes to speak again, but then stops as if he is on pause. I search his frozen features, touching his face to bring him back to me, before swinging my head around to find Grim watching.

"What are you doing?" I ask in a small voice, one I wish came out stronger. I pull myself away from Max and manage to stand. Grim's eyes fall on my bare chest, but I don't care. He can look all he fucking likes.

"You aren't meant to be here. We decided you aren't going to do this," I say again.

"He's sending people for you. They're almost here," he informs me, then he's gone.

I turn as Max starts moving again. His expression shows his confusion, and he says one word, "Death."

I only nod.

Chapter Eleven

He stands from his place at the base of the tree and hands me my shirt. I take it and put it on quickly, his silence making me uneasy. His mouth is set in a thin line, and he seems to be holding in his anger.

"You're angry," I say.

"Yes."

"Why?"

His jaw tics, and he grinds his teeth.

"Max," I say his name, and he answers me honestly.

"That he came at that time. That he saw you without your top on." He clenches his hands at his sides. "He has no right." I lay my hand on his arm, but the tension in his face doesn't ease.

"He came to warn me."

"Warn you about me?" Max asks.

"No. Viper knows I'm here and Death warned me he's sent people."

Max grabs me, picks me up, and quickly returns us to the camp. As soon as we get to my sister's door, he places me down, kisses my cheek, then takes off. While I stand there and gape after him, Tatiana opens the door.

"Why are you just standing out here?"

"Viper knows I'm here. Grim said people are coming." Her eyes go wide, and her daughter comes out and grips her leg. "You need to take all the vulnerable and hide."

"I don't hide," Tatiana states proudly.

I reach for her belly.

"You need to," I insist. "Not just for you."

John approaches, having heard what has just been said. "Lock yourself in the safe house." He picks up Tamika and hands her to Tatiana.

"I can help, though," Tatiana argues.

"You can, by keeping my family safe." He kisses her on the lips, and she nods before she turns back to me.

"Will you get Tanya? She needs to get to safety too, and so do you."

"I won't be coming..." She gives me a look, one that I know means she is about to argue. "... but I will get Tanya." Before I can leave, she captures my hand.

"I can't lose you twice. Don't get too close to Viper again."

I nod and go in search of Tanya. I find her and Melvon sitting at the table, eating when I walk in.

"You need to move. *Now.* Go to the safe house. Tatiana is waiting for you." Melvon instantly stands while Tanya sits there, staring at me.

"What? Why?"

"Viper has sent people." I hear a loud bang outside.

Melvon and I are immediately in motion. He picks up Tanya and is gone before I can say anything else.

When I step outside, about twenty vampires are surrounding the camp. Max's people are gone, but he is standing there with the wolves and a few of his guards beside him. I watch as a vampire runs at him, and as soon as it's close enough, his hand shoots out and grasps its neck. The shock on the vampire's face is evident—he didn't expect Max to be so fast. Max lifts him in the air and, in the next instant, squeezes him hard, and a loud snap is heard. He throws the vampire behind him, and one of his guards produces a spear and stabs the vampire directly in the heart. The others pause for moment, taking in what just transpired, but I watch on as if it's all happening in slow motion.

A smile creeps on their faces as John joins us. He stops next to me, checks me over, and strides over to where Max and his guards are standing.

"I wonder if your blood is going to be sweet or sour," a vampire hisses at Max.

Max says nothing back. He simply waits, looking nothing more than casual. As if he isn't worried by the vampire's threatening undertone.

One of the vampires spots me and smiles cruelly. Max glances back and sees me standing a little way off. My plan is if the vampires get past them, I'll be back here waiting to cut them off from getting to the others. I can't have them anywhere near my sisters.

So here I will stand and kill anyone who comes near me.

"The king wants you dead," one of them yells.

"Sounds familiar," I say, shrugging. "Queen, king." I smile. "Remember what happened to the last person you served."

"This one is different. His powers are natural, witch. He *will* kill you."

"Enough!" Max shouts, and all eyes turn to him. The vampires don't know who he is, but I watch as they become angered at the interruption. Vampires think they are above everyone and that we should never talk down to them.

How wrong they are.

They think because we are their food, we should respect them. It's another reason they serve whoever is in charge.

They like the power.

They have an appetite for it.

Power-hungry scum.

I despise power-hungry people because it always turns out the same way. It goes to their heads, and they think everyone should bow down to them.

Well, that needs to stop.

This all needs to stop.

Right now!

I step forward until I'm in line with Max and John, staring at the vampires. I feel it in my hands as the anger takes hold, and I know without a doubt I'm about to kill them.

"Wings." Valefar pops up in the middle of the vampires, his smile shining brightly as his gaze fixes on me. He moves closer, and Max places his hand in front to stop him. Valefar simply smiles and shakes his head. "I've come to collect on my deal, Wings. I've given you enough time."

"In case you didn't notice, we are in a bit of a predicament right now," I say to him. The vampires all glare as Valefar checks around before he focuses back on Max.

"He can handle them. They will all be dead before they can even blink." And before I can reply, Valefar grabs my arm, then suddenly we are no longer standing on the grass in front of the vampires.

"Where are we?" I demand.

"We are in the in-between."

"This is where *he* takes me," I whisper as I see the ocean. The night sky is bright and filled with stars.

"Yes. When he is here, we are not here. And vice versa."

"I didn't know what this place was."

"It was created from a memory. Of someone who once loved the beach, especially at night."

I sit on the sand and let my hands sift through it.

"My sisters..." I say, raising my eyes to his.

"Will be safe. Don't forget, they survived this long without you. A few more minutes in their time won't hurt them."

"Minutes?"

"Yes, time moves differently here." He walks over to me, pulls out the diary my sister gave him, and drops it to the ground at my feet. I reach for it and open to my mother's handwriting at the beginning. I trace my name as she mentions me.

"I wanted this for confirmation of what I already believe." His head drops to the side. "Why do you not look surprised?"

"By what?" I ask.

He tsks. "I can read almost anyone, Wings, and you are no exception. You know something."

"Do I?"

"You do, and I want the truth." I open the diary and start reading. She describes my powers, but my version of power is much more detailed than what is written.

"Truth?" I question, my eyes still on the diary's pages.

"Yes, Wings. I want the truth." He crouches down until he's on my level. "Are you the daughter of my father?" he asks.

"Your father?" My eyes snap to his, startled.

"You didn't really think I could be this powerful without having someone just as powerful in my blood-line, did you?" He shakes his head. "Lucifer is not known to produce heirs. I was his only one. But then I saw you one day, and I had this weird tingle." He drops his head, seemingly lost in the memory. "I thought to myself, *is she the same as me?*" Lifting his gaze to mine, he continues. "Your friend is part demon, that I know for sure. But his blood isn't the same as ours."

"Max."

"Yes..." He pauses. "You know, if they found out what you really are, they would never let you be queen. You would have to be a cruel queen, and I'm not sure you have that in you unless you are high. And let's be honest, no one likes demons. We like ourselves enough not to worry about what others think."

"You sure as shit like yourself enough for anyone," I retort.

"I like you just enough."

"That's sick. I could be your sister."

"We don't see a family like that. Family to demons is how we keep our bloodline strong and clean. And despite you being diluted, you are strong."

I stand and brush the sand from my pants. "Take me back," I demand.

"Give me the real diary," he replies, and I gawk at him. "You didn't think I didn't know, did you? I figured it out pretty quickly, but then you were gone. And we know your sister's only bargaining chip is you." I stare at him. "She may love your other sister, but she loves you much more."

"I want to go back. Take me back."

"You are a demon. Find your own way back." And then he is gone.

Fuck him.

Asshole.

Fuck!

Gosh, I love this whole swearing thing.

It doesn't feel evil to say bad words, as we were raised to believe.

I like it.

I think it's the new me.

That's why I tilt my head to the sky and yell, "You

motherfucking cocksucker... take. Me. Back!" I kick the sand and scream up at the stars.

"That mouth of yours got real dirty." I turn to find Grim standing there.

"Why are you here?" I ask, then rethink my words. "Take me back, please." I step toward him, but he steps away.

"Why are you here?" he asks instead.

"Because that awful demon brought me without permission."

"Why?"

"Because he thinks I'm his long-lost sister. Is that enough for you?"

"You are."

I freeze at his words.

"What did you say?"

"You have the same father. It's why he was always showing up."

"What's your excuse, then?" I ask, every feeling I have for him simmering inside me. He softens and enrages me in equal measures every time.

"I don't have an excuse. I was drawn to you, so I kept coming back. I will always come back for you, little fighter."

Goddamnit! I cover my ears as he says those two words.

"You can't say that to me, Grim. You can't push

me away and tell me we will never work, then say things like that. It confuses me," I tell him, swallowing down my rising emotions. I step closer, and when he doesn't move away again, I hold out my hand. "Please... take me back."

"As you wish." He takes hold of my hand and pulls me to him, our bodies now flush. There's no question he did that on purpose. As soon as I feel the air change, I know I am back.

Everything has stopped.

Max is kneeling on the ground, caring for someone.

John is on his way back to the house.

Pushing away from me, Grim leaves without another word.

Why must he do that to me?

Why?

I check around and see all the vampires are gone— ashes on the ground in their place—and know Max had a hand in their demise. Levy is sitting a short distance away, knowing she is safe with Max there.

That's what a good king or queen should do.

Make their people feel safe.

Time starts to move again, and as soon as it does, Max's head swings around, and his eyes find mine.

Chapter Twelve

Y*ou don't really plan to fall for two men, do you?*

Because I am falling for Max.

He is everything I should want.

Need.

There is no doubt in my mind we could be happy.

But there is also a part of me that screams for Grim.

How I wanted him with a force so fierce I was willing to sacrifice everything for him.

"Talia," Max says my name as he stands.

Valefar said time moves differently, yet it felt like I was gone for over an hour.

"How long was I gone?" I ask.

"Minutes," Max replies.

"But the vampires..."

"Dead." And I know he would have had no issues handling them all alone. "Are you okay? That demon didn't..." he trails off, not wanting to finish the sentence but wanting to know the answer.

I shake my head. "We aren't related, are we?" I ask Max. "Because even though demons don't mind keeping it in the bloodline, I do."

"My father was a low-level demon. Yours is not."

Okay! I nod.

That makes sense.

I think.

"Are you hurt?" he asks, reaching for me. I shake my head and pull back. "Did he bring you back?"

"No," I answer truthfully. "Who killed the vampires?"

"Me," he says, stepping even closer. "Then who brought you back?" This time when he reaches out to touch me, I let him because I am a sucker for all things Max.

"Valefar said I could do it myself, but I don't know how."

"You could. I can." My brows rise in surprise. "Did you not think I could?"

"No, I do. How do you do it?"

"I think of where I want to be, and I am there," he declares, as if it's that simple. It's not. I close my eyes and think of somewhere I want to be, and just as I do, Max squeezes me, and I open my eyes.

"It doesn't work like that for me," I tell him.

"No, it appears it does not."

"I wonder why. Maybe it's because you are part Angel as well."

"Possibly. But you are more powerful than me, so it should work for you."

I lean into him and rest my head on his shoulder. "I don't feel more powerful," I whisper.

"Talia." I turn to see John walking toward us. "Where did you go?"

"Valefar," I reply with a groan.

"Your sister needs you." I go to pull myself away from Max, but he holds me tighter.

"How did you get back?"

"Death," I say before I finally pull away from Max and leave without looking back.

"I think..." My sister starts pacing. She's back in her house and hasn't stopped moving back and forth, back and forth. "Oh my God." She bends over in pain, clutching her stomach.

"Tatiana." I run over to her and wrap an arm around her shoulders.

122

"Something isn't right... it doesn't feel right. It's too early." She gasps, and her free hand clutches mine. "Go and get John. I need John."

I run outside and see John already heading toward the house.

"Tatiana?" he asks, already guessing. "I felt..." He doesn't finish his sentence before he starts running toward the house. I rush after him to find Tatiana has her pants off and is bent down with her hands between her legs. Tears are streaming down her face as John holds her up.

"It's not right. It's not right..." she keeps repeating as she cries harder.

I walk over and stand next to her, not sure exactly what I can do. I've never helped deliver a baby, especially not one this early.

"John." He steps in front of her. "Can you hear a heartbeat?"

Before anyone can say anything, Grim appears.

Tatiana spots him at the same time I do.

"Grim..." I say his name, but his eyes are on my sister.

"No. No, not you. Go away. You can't have her." Tatiana's eyes are red now, she stops, and a scream rips from her mouth as she pushes harder. John leans down, and I watch as he pulls out the baby. He flips the tiny child around and smacks her back.

Smacks it and smacks it, trying to get her to breathe.

But nothing happens.

Grim steps closer.

Tears flow harder.

"Talia," my sister cries. She grabs her baby from John and falls to the floor, screaming my name again. "Make him go away. Please, make him go away."

My eyes fall to Grim.

He is watching.

He is waiting.

"Let me hold her," I say. My sister shakes her head, her tears continuing to stream heavily down her cheeks.

"He can't have her! I won't give her to him!" she screams. "He can't have her!" The whole house shakes from the force of her cries.

John is sitting next her, holding her tight, trying to provide comfort, though he's hurting just as badly.

"Give her to me," I say again.

When she doesn't answer, I reach down to take the baby. My sister lets her go and collapses back into John's arms.

I look down at her tiny form and feel Grim getting closer. I step back, holding her close, and without thinking, I lean down and kiss her forehead. Then I whisper to her, "Just a small part of me." And I let my breath go.

"Little fighter, no."

But it's too late.

I did it.

And a small cry leaves the baby in my arms.

My sister stands and reaches for the baby, taking her from my hold as I fall to the floor.

"You don't know what you just did," Grim says while looking down at me. "You aren't allowed to meddle with death. I was being nice and not taking her because of you, little fighter. And this is what I get."

"She's alive!" I scream, now on my hands and knees.

Death drops down, so we are nose to nose.

"And when you die, she will as well." Then he is gone.

The room falls silent.

Did he just...

"What did he just say?" my sister says, no longer screaming. "Did he..." She shakes her head.

"That can't be right," John says as the door opens. I'm too tired to check who it is. But then my body is lifted, and I'm scooped into familiar arms.

"I'm removing you."

"Stop. She just—" John places his hand on Max's arm.

"You will remove your hand from me, and you will not stop me from taking her. She sacrificed herself for your daughter. The babe should have died, yet here she is. Let Talia go."

"Talia." I turn my head from Max's chest to look at my sister. "Thank you. Thank you so much." I offer her a small smile before Max strides out of the house.

"You shouldn't have done that," Max scolds.

"How do you know what I did?"

"Death." I lay my head on his bicep. "I almost ripped his head off, but then he said what you did. And when he told me, I knew he hated doing that. I didn't even wait for him to finish before I found you."

"It's a baby," I argue.

"And now that baby is joined to you."

"I didn't know what I was doing."

"Do you plan to take her with us?" I hear Levy ask.

Max stops, and I don't even bother turning to face her. "If Talia wants to go with me, I'll take her anywhere." I smile at his voice before my eyes become heavy, but I hear what she says.

"If she goes, I won't." And I can just imagine her crossing her arms over her chest as she says it. "You can have *me*. We don't need *her*."

Max walks away without replying.

* * *

When I wake, my body is warm, and I feel better. Not so drained. Stretching my legs, I move, only to feel the reason I'm warm is because I have someone next to me. Our legs are entwined, and a soft snore leaves him.

Scanning the area around me, I see we are in his tent. He's the only one who doesn't share with anyone else, but he's still close to his people. When I go to move, he reaches out and pulls me straight back to him. His arms circle me, and I lay my head on his chest.

"Did you dream of me?" he asks, not opening his eyes.

"I dreamt of nothing," I tell him. "It was quiet."

"I dreamed of you," he says as he opens his eyes. "I'm leaving today, and I want you to come with me."

I stay still, not really sure how to reply to those words. I've been away from my family before, and I didn't enjoy it, but I will admit it feels different this time. Both my sisters have created families of their own while I'm still stuck in this limbo. I always imagined that it would be just us three sisters, though sometimes I added Grim to the image. But then when I got older and realized that just isn't the way this world works, and what was a short time away for me was a long time for them. We are still the same, but we are now somewhat different.

Tatiana has two children of her own and a man who will never leave her side. And Tanya only seems to see Melvon, which is okay because it works for them.

"You shouldn't stay where the child is. You know it's risky. Your sister will try to stop you from doing anything that could harm the baby."

I bite my lip as I listen to him breathe.

He's right. My sister has always been protective of me, and I'm not one of her children. So her protection for her own child will be a force to be reckoned with. I turn to look at Max and find him watching me with sleepy eyes.

"I'd like to kiss you," I tell him.

Then, in one swift movement, he picks me up, so my body is lying on his.

"So kiss me, pretty."

"Pretty?" I smile at him.

"Yes, it's what you are. Pretty, intelligent, and strong, amongst many other things. But pretty"—he brushes my hair from my face—"is the one I favor the most right now. Especially as those mossy-green eyes stare back at me."

I do as he asks with absolutely no hesitation whatsoever. Kissing Max has become one of my favorite things. So I lean in, my lips hovering above his, teasing him. But Max is used to getting what he wants—he is a king, after all.

His hands frame my face, and he tucks the loose hair behind each ear before he pulls me a little bit farther down, and our lips touch. It's soft at first and all-consuming, just a simple kiss from unpretentious lips. My tongue slides out and licks over his lips, and he opens instantly.

Lying atop, I feel every inch of him harden below me. And I can't help but move my body like it's been electrified, and every part of it is on fire, wanting and needing to be extinguished but in the most exhilarating of ways. And I know for a fact he can do exactly that.

He breaks our kiss as he pulls my head back.

"Are you sure?" he asks, knowing what I need without any declaration.

I simply smile before I sit up and pull my shirt from my body. Max lifts one hand, cups my breast, and massages before tweaking my nipple. Lifting away to stand above him, I shove my pants down my legs. At first, he doesn't move. He simply lies there watching me. But as soon as I'm completely naked, he sits up and, with one hand, he pulls off his shirt, throws it to the side, then tugs me straight back down.

Our lips find each other again, and those very same hands that were holding my face skim down the sides of my body until they reach my ass. He grips it with both hands, squeezes, then smacks my ass. Hard.

I yelp, and I feel him smile against my lips.

"Are you a virgin?" he asks.

"No," I answer, and he flips me to my back, so he's hovering over me.

"Good, that means we don't have to take it easy."

"Easy?" I murmur, lost in the lust that's overtaking me.

When he smirks, it's full of promises that I know he will deliver. I've been with two men in my life—one didn't know how to find my clit, and the other, I was so lost in, that I think I was willing to accept the bare minimum.

I won't do that anymore.

If I give myself to someone, I want everything in return. A fair exchange. And I have a feeling Max will try to give me everything I could ever think to want.

I just wish the same could be said for Grim.

Is it possible to love two men at the same time? I'm not entirely sure, but I have a feeling that's exactly where I'm headed. And I'm not going to complain about it, either.

One is always going to be a mystery, while the other is currently leaning down and biting my breast, lavishing me with his full attention. He takes my nipple into his mouth, then pops it out and does the exact same to the other. I lift my hips so I can feel him between my legs, even though he's still wearing his trousers, and he meets me halfway.

I start to grind against him, and his hands find mine, pinning them above my head and securing them together in a tight yet gentle grip. His other hand skirts down my body until it reaches the top of my pussy. He slides through my folds and easily slips a finger into my core. Though I fight to keep it trapped, a moan escapes between my lips. His mouth is still working on each breast, sometimes wandering up to my neck, only to suck and kiss his way back down to my pebbled nipples.

I've never been in this position before, giving someone full control of my body. I was taught that my body is a vessel and only I know it best, but Max sure as shit knows what he's doing and I'm not sure I ever want to stop him.

"Tell me, pretty, do you want my mouth on you?" I'm stunned by his question, but nod anyway. "What your sweet pussy wants, it gets." He presses another kiss to each nipple before he stands and removes his trousers. And when he's fully bare, I'm met with a large cock. *Holy shit.*

That's going to hurt.

A lot.

Chapter Thirteen

Max lowers down to his knees and smiles.

"I'm going to enjoy tasting you. Tell me, pretty, does this sweet cunt want what I can give it?" His use of the vulgar language we were taught not to use edges me on. And everything inside of me lights up.

"I don't know, you tell me." I sit up on my elbows and stare at him. "Can you make me come?"

He growls before he pushes me back and leans over my body, his blue eyes shining back at me with a look that has me squirming.

"Let's make a deal. You scream, and I'll stop."

"What if it's a good scream?"

He smirks. "Oh, I know it's going to be a good scream." *Cocky much?* "If you touch my hair, I'll stop."

"What? Why?" I ask him.

"Because when you hold my hair, I want it to be when I'm buried deep within that sweet pussy of yours. Now, throw up a silencing spell. You don't want the world to know how loud I can make you come, now, do you?" My head drops back, and I do as he asks, humming the spell and smiling.

He wastes no time before I feel his mouth touch me there.

Every part of me ignites. He kisses my pussy the same way he kisses my lips—slow and deliberate—until his tongue finds its way in and hits that perfect spot. My hands are fisted at my sides as he continues to slide his tongue up and down, up and down, circling my clit before using his whole mouth and licking, then finally sliding in a finger followed by a second.

Max whispers, "You taste like heaven."

And somehow his words make my hips thrust against his mouth. My hands twitch, wanting to bury themselves in his hair, but I quickly dig my fingers into the sheets beside me, remembering what he said about touching. I bite my lip as I feel myself coming, and he slides in another finger, keeping the perfect pace, not picking up and not slowing down, pushing me right through my release with the good kind of scream.

I could imagine myself doing this with him endlessly. To have him always touching me would be a pleasure as well as a curse because I wouldn't want him to stop.

He rolls us over, so he's on his back, then picks me up as if I weigh nothing, holding me above him.

"You listened," he says.

"Do I get a reward?" He lowers me just a little until the tip of his cock is at my entrance.

"Reward? Did I not just give you one?"

"You did." I smile. "And I quite enjoyed it."

He lowers me again, and he slips a little more inside, driving a whimper from my lips.

It's torture.

Sweet, sweet torture.

"I would like to be your first everything."

"Do you?" I lean down and give him a quick kiss, and he lowers me just a bit more.

"I do, and I don't like sharing."

"Well, don't share me, then."

Max nods and slowly lowers me one last time until I am seated on him. I squirm at the feeling of him inside me, moaning into his mouth. It feels good. Full, but good. He doesn't move, just lets me get comfortable before I raise my hips just a little.

"Tell me when I can move." He breathes out, watching me. His hands grip my hips, getting ready to thrust. But I ignore him and start rolling my hips instead, sliding up and down, taking him in.

He growls, and I know he's holding back. So I keep on going, revelling in how his hands grip harder on my sides.

I vaguely hear someone call out my name, but we ignore them.

I get close to his ear. "Do you want to move?" I whisper, and he simply nods. "What if I said you weren't allowed?" My hips don't stop their sultry dance.

"I would still die a happy man."

"Angel-demon, I think you meant to say." My hands grip his shoulders to get better traction, and my hips bounce faster.

"Yes," he replies back, but I have already forgotten what I said.

"Maxilliam," I say his full name, drawing it out as I clench around his length.

"You don't call me that!" he growls, then leans in and bites my neck. "You call me Max. The others call me that, but never you."

I nod and whisper in his ear, "You can move now."

I could say I'd forgotten how fast he is, but I don't. In a flash, he's standing, remaining hard and deep inside me. His hands cup my ass, and he slides a finger into my hole as he bounces me on his cock. I grip on for dear life and feel my orgasm building straight away.

Granted, I was already riding and teasing him, but fuck.

He growls as I bury my fingers in his hair and pull. He doesn't care, not once breaking his rhythm.

He fucks me.

Fucks me.

And fucks me.

Until somehow, we're back on the ground, with him still inside of me as I come.

Again.

"We aren't done," he says as my arms fall limply to my sides.

"I need... rest," I pant through a laugh, trying to catch my breath.

My sister calls my name.

Max reaches for a sheet and pulls it over us as he answers her. "Yes, she's in here."

The tent door opens, and Tatiana stands there, her eyes still red. "We need to talk." It's then that she realizes what we were doing as her eyes go wide, and she blushes. I nod, and she makes a hasty exit, closing the tent and leaving.

I sit up and reach for my clothes.

"You shouldn't go," Max says.

I stand, sliding my pants on.

"Why?"

"I can smell her motives, and they aren't right. The

sister you knew, who would protect you over everything, is not there right now."

I shake my head. He can't know that, I should know my sister better then anyone.

"She is," I insist. I know my sister better than he does. Max has only just met her.

"No, she isn't." I step out of the tent and when I look back, he is watching me.

"I'm leaving today. You should come with me."

I walk off without another word and am stopped by Levy. "You shouldn't come with us. You had your taste. Now let us go in peace."

I push past her, not even bothering to reply. There is no point antagonizing her. She will have to get used to Max and me being together at some stage, but right now is not the time.

As soon as I arrive at my sister's house, I open the door to find the mess cleaned up and Tatiana, Tanya, and John sitting around the table. They all glance at me when I enter, Tatiana with the baby in her arms. I step closer to look at her, but notice my sister hold her a little tighter.

"Do you know what you did?" Tatiana asks.

"What I did?"

Tears fall down her cheeks. "Not only will I lose you if you die, but I'll also lose her." Her gaze falls on the baby. John sits there silently while Tanya quietly plays with her nails.

"I was just trying to help."

"And I thank you for what you did. I'm not sure where I would be if I lost her." John reaches out and lays a hand on her arm, but she doesn't acknowledge him. "Max is leaving, but you need to stay."

I pull out a chair and sit at the table with them. "Why?"

"Because I can't have you out there defending them. I need you here where I know what to expect."

"You won't be able to protect me from everything," I tell her. "And I won't be locked away here either." I stand, shaking my head. "I'm not a prisoner, Tatiana, least of all yours."

Her sharp eyes find mine. "What's that meant to mean?"

"It means that you are my sister, not my warden."

She rears her head back at my words. "I will do whatever is necessary to protect what's mine."

"And you can, but I am *not* yours."

I turn to leave, but I hear her chanting a spell. No one does anything to stop her, and when I turn back around, I see Tanya has her head down, and John is watching Tatiana.

Her eyes go vibrant green, and I see the spell forming—it's one that would bind me to the house. I storm over to her, and as she gets to the last verse, I snatch the spell away from her and break it.

Everyone stops breathing.

"How?"

I don't know how I did that, but I could see like it was a bubble that just needed to be popped. So that's what I did.

"You will *never* do that to me again. Do you hear me?" I state.

John stands, and I spin toward him. "If you try anything, John, I will put you down."

"Talia," Tanya says. "This needs to stop. She just wants you safe, so in return, the baby is safe."

"I'll work out a way to break the spell, but I'm not staying here while I do that."

"You can't break it," John says firmly.

"I couldn't do a lot of things, yet here I am." I throw my hands up and grab our mother's diary from the table, which is open to the spell I used on the baby. It says that the spell can't be broken, but there is a note that she had never tried the spell, so that means there could be a way around the issue. I put the diary under my arm and walk out the door. As soon as the door is shut behind me, I head straight to Max's tent.

I hate that he was right.

That he saw what was about to happen before I did.

How he felt it.

I bump into someone, and my head rises to find Max staring down at me.

Except his face is unreadable.

"What's wrong?" I ask, reaching for him, but he pushes my hand away.

"We are leaving, and it's best you don't come," he states.

"I..." I shake my head, not fulling understanding. "You said I should come."

"I take it back. It's too dangerous with you. My job is to keep everyone safe."

"Wow, okay." I step back, and he makes no move to follow me. I turn and head for the same tree I kissed him under, then drop down under it, bringing my knees up and wrapping my arms around them. I'm unsure how his feelings could change so fast, and why did I not fight it?

"Valefar." I call his name and within a few seconds, he appears.

"Yes, Wings."

"Does he know of me?" He knows who I'm talking about.

"I'm not sure." He shrugs. "Should we find out?"

I nod and offer him my hand. He takes it and pulls me to my feet. I glance past him to Max, who's watching us. He opens his mouth to say something, but in the next breath, I am gone.

I shouldn't have trusted him.

He got what he wanted and then disposed of me as if I am nothing.

I am *not nothing*.

I am Talia.

And I *am* a *powerful witch*.

A powerful witch who's about to meet her father and is shitting her pants just thinking about it.

Chapter Fourteen

"Where are we?" I ask Valefar.

We are in a nondescript sitting area with cream-colored walls. Chairs are grouped in circles, and colorful demonic paintings hang on the walls.

"This is his domain. Only high-level demons can enter." I turn to face him. "And his children, which should only be me..." He winks as the doors open, and a man steps in. He stops when he sees Valefar, and then his red gaze focuses directly on mine.

"I would recognize those eyes anywhere." In the next instant, he is directly in front of me. He lifts his hand and touches my hair, but I step away. "You are your mother's daughter."

"And yours, it seems," Valefar states.

The demon in front of me—who I might add is

handsome, dressed in a clean black suit, shiny black shoes, and slicked-back, dark hair—turns away from me to address Valefar.

"You went searching for her."

"Yes, Lucifer, your secret child has been found."

Lucifer steps up to Valefar, and I watch as he backhands him across the face. Hard.

Valefar doesn't even flinch. "Did that make you feel better?" he snarls before he disappears, leaving me alone with Lucifer.

I'm frozen in place as Lucifer spins around to face me. "Where were we?" he says and goes to a seat. He waves his hand, indicating for me to sit as well, so I do.

I'm unsure what to say or do. I cross my legs over each other as he watches me.

"You'll have to excuse Valefar. He has a jealousy issue. He'll realize the longer he is on this earth that it's unnecessary to hold on to stupid ideas."

"And is that where we are on this earth?" I ask, scanning the room.

"No, daughter. We are in Hell." He smiles, showing incredibly white teeth. "It's amazing how much you look like her." Lucifer sits back and snaps his fingers, and a drink appears in his hand. He holds it up and asks, "Want one?"

I shake my head, and he puts it to his lips, taking a sip.

"You are nervous. Why?" he asks.

"It's not every day you meet the Devil and find out he's your father."

"The Devil. Haven't been called that in a long time. I would like to say I run Hell. Is that so hard?" My head drops to the side as I study him. "Tell me, do you have my powers?"

"Powers?" I question him.

"You see, your mother hid you from me with a protection spell. I didn't even know of your existence until she died. But I was biding my time before I came to you. Things needed to be done. And as you are aware, I am a person who gets things done where I am from. It was only a matter of time before I went looking." He takes another sip from his drink. "And then I did go looking. And you weren't there any longer, so I presumed you dead."

"Viper sent me through me a portal."

"Viper, yes. I'm waiting for his soul to come and visit me. Don't worry, daughter, I'll torture him for eternity for what he did to you."

Right! Okay! I'm not sure if I want to say thank you, but then he sits up and snaps his fingers, and someone falls to the floor next to me. When I glance down, I see matted, long hair covering their face as they kneel. "Just as I am doing to this one for what she did to you."

The figure looks up, and I see Veronica staring back at me. She is dressed in ratty clothes, and her face is filthy. She recognizes me immediately and snarls.

"Now, now, sweet thing, you want to go back to the cage?" Lucifer taunts, and Veronica instantly stops and bows her head. Glancing back at Lucifer, I see him smiling. "Slit her throat. Quite poetic, wouldn't you say?"

"She deserves it after what she did," I bite back.

"Yes, to the wolf." I look back to Veronica, who is keeping her head low. "It's okay. She is paying for her sins. And the colorful language she spouts at me is quite hilarious."

"Asshole," she mutters, and he ignores her. But she does look up and stare at me. "I knew you were the devil. I would have been a better queen than you. I *was* a better queen."

"But she isn't queen," Lucifer says. "Yet."

"What a waste," Veronica mutters before he waves his hand, and then she is gone.

"She is a waste of space, only a lick of power, and held so much. You, my dear, are different."

"I don't want to be queen," I tell him.

"But you will be."

"Who says?"

"Well, the prophecy, of course, and that never lies."

He shakes his head. "But back to your mother. Did she ever tell you?"

"No."

He seems to think about that for a few moments.

"It was forbidden for me to take someone on earth, but sometimes I would pop up and wander around. I like the smell, you see. I had been doing it for centuries, and no other human had ever caught my attention until her. It was the eyes... those green eyes, that held me so. She was by herself near a river. I watched her for days as she would come and try to move the water. You see, your mother was an earth witch, but she loved the water just the same." He watches me the whole time he speaks.

"I know what type of witch she was."

"Do you have earth powers?"

"I have all," I whisper.

He claps his hands.

"Splendid. She would greatly approve," he says, then he continues his story. "One day, I decided it would be fun to play a trick on her. What I didn't count on was how clever she was. And at the time, she already had two children, and I don't think she wanted a third. And I certainly didn't want another child.

"Anyway, I played with her. I lifted the water at her spell, and at first, shock registered on her face as though she thought it was she who had conjured the movement. But witches only have an affinity for one element unless, of course, they are you." He bows his head.

"But she was clever, and she realized it wasn't her doing it. I left before she could see me, but I came back, day after day, and repeated the conjuring. She looked for me every time. Sometimes she would bring her two kids. Others, it was just her alone." He takes another long drink, and I watch as the glass refills itself. "We did this song and dance for almost a year until one day, she started yelling, and I knew it was directed at me.

"You see, we don't have the same desires as you. Yes, we are demons, and we love lust... *fucking,* as you like to put it. But nothing more. Ever."

I go to speak, but he continues. "Until her."

"She was beautiful," I say.

"She was more than beautiful, child. She was magnificent," he says a little wistfully. "I had played with her for so long that I decided it was time to finally meet her. And on that day, she didn't have her children with her—it was just her by herself, screaming at the top of her lungs. I don't think she was expecting me, of all people, to appear. Actually, I'm not even sure she knew who I was at first, but she knew I was powerful all the same.

"Your mother had a rare gift. She could smell

power a mile away. She could tell you what someone's gift was and describe it to you in detail. When she started describing mine, I sat there watching her in complete fascination that she knew the tricks up my sleeve that no one else could possibly realize."

He takes another drink and leans forward. "I tried to kiss her that first day, and she slapped my face and told me she was already spoken for." He smiles at the memory. "But I continued to show up every day after, and so did she. I don't think she understood what game she was playing with me and what a dangerous game it was.

"I kissed your mother for the first time a year after meeting her. It wasn't long after that I had her, and not once did she mention a partner again when she came to visit me, nor did she speak of where her girls were."

I smile, thinking of her talking about them.

"We continued to sneak away to see each other and steal kisses through the night. She never once asked me who I was, but I think she knew in the end. I remember the last night I saw her. I had a feeling she was pregnant, but I couldn't be sure if it was mine or the other children's father, so I didn't question it.

"She called things off"—he pauses like it causes him pain—"and told me she would never visit me again and for me to never try to contact her. I am the King of Hell, it's not like I take no for an answer. So when she did stop showing up, I remember visiting her without her knowledge, but I think she knew. Because, as I said, your mother was incredibly good at smelling power.

"She was heavily pregnant with you, and a part of me knew that you were my child. The other part didn't want to acknowledge the fact, as I already had one child, and he was a handful, so I left, and never returned. It was easy as that. I figured the day she would die, I would see her again, as she did sin with me after all. But your mother is as pure as snow, and not even I could have her for eternity. The gods would not be that kind."

I sit quietly, watching him talk of her in the way of someone whom he once loved and lost, but he says he cannot love. I wonder how true that statement actually is.

"Do you miss her?"

"That is fickle, wouldn't you say? Missing someone when you are incapable of love?"

"No, I would not say. I miss her deeply and wish I had more time with her."

"You look just like her."

"We all do," I tell him. "My sisters and I, that is."

"Yes, I remember them." He stands and smiles. "Come, let me show you something."

"Should I trust you?" I ask knowing full well it's

the silliest question to the ask the devil, but I do anyway.

Lucifer throws his head back and laughs. "Ah, sweet girl, you should never trust anyone." He leans in and whispers, "Ever." Then he proceeds to walk out of the room, and I follow.

I shouldn't trust anyone?

I trust my sisters.

Don't I?

At least, I think I do.

We enter another room, and this one is full of pictures. They're of him and my mother. There are so many of them scattered everywhere. I reach for one, skimming my finger over her face, and warmth blooms in my chest.

"You can have it." I look over my shoulder to find him watching me. "Cameras became a thing of the past as the centuries went on, but I always loved the device and kept it. I introduced it to your mother, and she also fell in love with the contraption and would take endless photos of everything, including me." He smiles.

"Aren't you meant to be bad?" I ask, completely thrown off by everything happening right now.

"Oh, I am, sweet girl. The worst. There is literally no one worse than me. Though my son may come in a close second, but it seems he has taken a liking to you. Tell me, do you have that effect on most people?"

"Effect?" I ask, my brows drawing together in confusion.

"Yes, are people drawn to you?"

"I'm not sure. Maybe? Possibly? No?" I don't have a straight answer for him.

"What powers do you possess?" he asks.

I hold the photograph of my mother and look at him. "Do you plan to steal them?" I inquire.

He smirks. "No. But by that, I know you also have that power, which not even Valefar has. Interesting." He taps his jaw as if he's thinking. "What else?"

"We discovered I can open a portal with enough juice, but my own power is not enough."

"We?" he asks, leaning in.

"Yes, his name is Maxilliam."

"King Maxilliam?" he asks. My brows scrunch, and I nod my head.

"Interesting. I had heard stories of a man with both Angel and demon blood, but I would not have believed it. This King Maxilliam... did you kill him when you took his power?"

"No. He is strong."

"Good. Strong is what you are going to need. Soon, people will know where you come from. It's only a matter of time..." He pauses, a proud smile spreading across his face. "You *will* be queen."

"I don't want to be queen," I tell him, almost whining. "When are people going to understand that?" I shake my head with a huff. "I have a question."

He waits for me to go on.

"Why can't I move through time like you?"

His brows pinch. "You should absolutely be able to move through time," he replies. "Without a doubt."

"Valefar does it, and Max said all I have to do is think of where I want to be."

He laughs at my words. "No, sweet girl. You and I do no such thing. We can't just think where we want to be... we have to *be*." He reaches for me, and in the next instant, we are standing in front of a lake. "This is where I met your mother."

I've never been here before. Cardia is large, and I traveled a lot of it lately, but this is one place I haven't seen.

"You can't just think... *you* need to *be*. I want to be here... and to be here, I felt it with every fiber of my being, darkness and all. It takes me less than a second now to be where I want." He pauses. "I can go places Valefar cannot, but I have a feeling you are going to be the same." He touches my face, covers my eyes, and he says, "Tell me where you want to be and why."

"I want to see Max," I blurt out the words before

thinking clearly.

"Now... where do you want to be?" he asks again.

"With Max," I gush out.

"Open your eyes."

I do and find we are standing in front of Max and all his people. They appear worse for wear, but I notice they made it through Viper's forest.

"How many days has it been?" I whisper, and that's when Max notices me standing there. His eyes go wide, and he starts toward me. As he gets halfway, I watch as Levy puts her hand out and blocks him from reaching me. He halts, and she speaks, "She left you. Remember that. And look, she shows up with another man." I say nothing while Max stands there, unsure of what is happening.

"You told me to stay, that you didn't want me to join you," I whisper, and his brows pinch. Before we can say anything more, Lucifer moves and returns in a blink, standing next to me, but this time, he isn't alone. No, he is standing there holding a shrieking Levy.

"Do you care to tell my daughter what you did?"

"Get your hands off me, demon!" she shouts, but Lucifer only laughs, and that laugh is satanic in nature.

"I am not a demon! I am the fucking king of demons, so watch your words before I slice your tongue from your mouth."

I gape at Lucifer, not knowing exactly what to say.

"Remove your hand," Max says, now standing in front of us.

"Tell him," Lucifer commands, squeezing down harder on her neck. "Or I will end you right here, right now, and take you to Hell with me to play."

"I shifted into you," Levy admits to Max on a pathetic cry. "I didn't want *her* to come, so I told *her* when I was you that you didn't want *her* to come."

My mouth hangs open at her words.

"She is the reason you left?" Max asks, looking at me.

"No, I thought *you* were," I tell him.

"I would never leave you willingly. It's been weeks. I never thought I would see you again."

"This is cute and all, but I must really be going," Lucifer says simply and turns to me. "When you need me, remember to *be*." He looks to Levy, who's still in his grip. "And you, my dear, are coming with me." He snaps her neck, and I watch as her lifeless body falls to the ground. Grim appears, and his surprised expression stuns me.

"Hello, old friend," Lucifer says, but Grim is looking at me.

"Oh, I see." Lucifer grabs hold of me again, and we are gone.

Chapter Fifteen

We reappear in the sitting room of Lucifer's domain. Valefar is seated in the chair where Lucifer sat earlier and glances up at our entrance.

"Fancy seeing you two again. Bonding, I hope?"

I push away from Lucifer. "You killed her," I say in shock.

"I did. She betrayed you. You have to be a cruel queen to rule this world."

"Why does everyone keep saying that? I do *not* need to be *cruel.*"

"But you do," Valefar interjects. "No one nice can hold a throne."

Lucifer walks over to his son.

"Grim." He says the name, and Valefar looks at me. "So, the rumors are true. He has fallen for an earth woman." Lucifer spins around. "Never thought I would see the day..."

"He hasn't. We aren't a thing," I tell him.

"That Angel has been saving you, correct?" Lucifer asks.

"Correct."

"He knows what you are, but never shared it with you." I nod through a rough swallow, wanting to leave right this second. "Interesting. I wonder if he was afraid of what you might do if you knew. Too late for that now, I suppose."

"I'm leaving." I close my eyes, intending to think of Max, but Grim pops into my head instead, and somehow, I end up in the in-between, and I find him staring out at the ocean. He knows I'm here and turns around slowly. When his silver eyes lock on mine, I'm not sure what to do.

I shouldn't be here.

I should be with Max.

Yet, I came here.

Why?

"You know." It isn't a question.

"I know," I confirm.

He takes a step toward me, and my heart rate picks up the closer he gets. He stops when he reaches me and cups my cheek in his palm. "I was interested at first... the very first time I visited you. I wanted to know if the rumors were true. They couldn't be, though, right? Lucifer doesn't mix with earthly people. But when I saw her and then you, I knew it was all true. You were *his* daughter. You have *his* power as well as your mother's. You were going to change this world and make it a better place."

I can't help but lean into his touch. "I didn't choose to be like this."

"I know. It's what makes you all that more special. You always thought your power would be better off in your sister's hands. But you are wrong. While she is strong, she isn't you. You hold qualities no one else possesses. And that is a miracle within itself."

"She hates me now."

"No, she is scared of you. There is a difference. She realizes what value your life is even more."

"I hate it," I whisper. "I don't want it."

"I'm sorry, but not even I can change that." He closes his eyes briefly, then looks back at me, and I see it in his gaze before he says the words. "It has been a pleasure knowing you, little fighter. You showed me things no one else ever could." He leans down and touches his lips to mine. It's a soft and tender kiss, and when I pull back, Grim looks over my shoulder. I follow his gaze to see Max standing there, watching me intently. In the next blink, he's gone.

I shove Grim's hand away. "Did you know he would come?" I ask, stepping back.

"Yes," and then he's gone too. My hands start to sweat, nerves take hold as I think where I should be.

I think of Max and where I want to be, and I am suddenly standing in front of him. He's pacing back and forth, with his people as they set up in tents as the night falls.

Max stops when he spots me. "You let him kiss you," he growls. "Touch you," he says through his teeth.

"He was saying goodbye," I tell him.

"He will *never* say goodbye, not to someone like you."

"What's that meant to mean?"

He waves his hand in the air. "We buried Levy," he says. "I didn't know she did that. How could you think, after what we did, I would not want you with me?"

"I forgot what she could do. I just..." I shake my head, not knowing how to answer him. I feel so ridiculous to have thought he'd treat me that way. "I didn't know."

"I would *never* tell you to go, Talia. Ever." He reaches for me and lifts me up effortlessly into his arms. Holding me tightly to him, I wrap my legs firmly around his waist.

"You are mine, for now, and forever. And if Death thinks he has a chance, I'll introduce him to his own untimely demise," he says before his lips find mine. He kisses me passionately, and it takes my breath away.

I hate to compare the two.

But I do.

Grim kisses me slowly, more deliberate.

Max kisses me with a force so intense that I know every need he has is primal, and he wants every piece of me.

Even the bad.

When I'm in Max's arms, he helps me forget all the little things, and I can't say that I don't turn to mush beneath his touch. He starts walking with me, not breaking the kiss and gripping hold for dear life. He doesn't let me go until he lowers himself to the ground and slowly puts me down, so he is on his knees, hovering above me.

"I need you. I need to claim you." His words are unsure, like he's afraid they might scare me away.

I nod my head, lift up, and pull my shirt off over my head. "I'm yours. Take me, Max."

Not wasting any time, he grabs my hips, tugging my pants down, stripping me bare. His chest rumbles as he looks at me writhing before him, needing more of his touch and feeling entirely on display. Pressing another kiss to my lips, he turns me over, so I'm on my hands and knees. Then he slaps my ass. He does it once, then twice, before his next slap lands on my pussy. I am wet for him and know full well that I would let him take me or, as he so accurately puts it, claim me any time and anywhere he wanted.

"This sweet, sweet cunt is mine. Isn't it, pretty?"

His fingers slide between my ass cheeks until they reach my pussy, where he pushes a finger inside me while his other fingers play with my clit. I'm ready for him and push back into his hand, hearing my wetness as I go. He groans as I fuck his fingers. I can't stop, my rhythm picking up, and just as I feel myself build, he pulls away. I moan loudly at the loss before he shushes me.

"It's okay, pretty. This sweet cunt of yours is screaming for my cock. I just had to get you all good and wet for me. I want to feel your cunt milking my cock, and you will scream my fucking name when you come. Do you hear me? No one else's will leave those pretty lips."

And before I can respond, I feel him at my entrance. He drives into me nice and slow, his hands on my hips taking full control. And I let him because I like the power he excites in me.

It's intoxicating.

He is intoxicating.

And I'm drunk from everything he is.

I thought the only high I could reach was when I took someone's power, but how wrong I was. Max delivers me to a different high, and I completely understand the power of sex and all that it holds, especially when it's with someone who knows exactly what they are doing. And believe me when I say Max knows precisely what he's doing with his cock and with my pussy.

"You feel that, pretty? You feel how good we are together?"

"Yes!" I scream, and he slaps my ass before he grips me again, moving faster. His hand comes around and rubs my clit, giving me all the friction I need to bring me right to the edge.

Max is incredible.

And I'm here for it.

Every second of it.

Is there a world where you can fuck all the time? If so, I want to visit it and book a permanent stay.

"Those lips will only ever touch mine again, correct?" he growls, and I can only nod in answer, but he slaps my ass. "Say it."

"Yes, Max."

"That's my good pretty."

He fucks me hard and fast, brutally and beautifully.

And as I come, he doesn't slow down. Max holds

me up when I can no longer do so myself, and I feel a second orgasm cresting before I can even catch a breath. He doesn't stop, and I'm not sure I want him to. I feel it when he comes, my own release exploding at the same time. His hands grip my hair, and he pulls my head back as he rides me through our pleasure.

Once we're both spent, he stands, as if invigorated, dresses with a smile, then dresses me gently, all while I lie limply on the ground, unable to move. When my clothes are righted, he picks me up and carries me to his tent, then he settles me inside with a kiss to my head before he leaves. I curl up in a ball, ready to pass out, when he comes back with a bowl full of food.

"Eat. I need you strong."

I do as he asks, not having to be told twice.

Max sits opposite me, feeding me each piece of fruit before he also takes his own bites. We sit in silence, as sometimes words are simply not needed. And with him, the moment feels like bliss.

When I'm done, he takes my face in his hands and kisses me until I'm breathless, telling me he'll be back and to dream of him.

I'm exhausted, but it's a long time before I pass out and do just that.

And it's the most peaceful night of sleep I can remember having.

* * *

Loud noises wake me, echoing all around me. Before I can even think better of it, I'm out of the tent and heading straight toward the commotion. I spot the source immediately—Tanya and Melvon are standing with Max, arguing to see me.

Tanya spots me and calls out my name.

Max whips his gaze to mine and shakes his head. "She isn't going with you," he tells them.

"What are you, her keeper?" my sister asks with her hands on her hips. Melvon is quiet at her side. She pushes past him and comes directly to me, grabbing me by the shoulders and checking me over. "You didn't come back. Why didn't you come back?"

"You know why," I tell her, pulling away.

"She would never hurt you."

"I don't think she can hurt me, Tanya, but she will try anything for her daughters."

"I want you to come back. She asked that I bring you back, where it's safe."

"It's not safe *anywhere*." That's when I look around and realize we are in a quadrant, a place where we once shopped for food and anything we could afford. What once was a thriving market is now next to nothing. "But I don't plan to go back there."

"Where do you plan to go?" she asks, her voice

growing more frantic. "Here?" She waves her hand around the quadrant. "This is nowhere. You are going nowhere."

"We are going to the castle." We both turn at Max's voice. He has a determined look on his face. "We will talk to your king. If he doesn't let us stay, I'll have no choice but to end him."

"He won't let you stay," Tanya says without hesitation. "Least of all with her." She nods her head in my direction.

"You may be right, but Talia is mine now. It's done, and no one can break that bond."

I look at him, a little bewildered.

What does that mean?

Is he merely saying that for the sake of saying it?

That's not like him. What he says, he always means.

"You claimed her?" Tanya asks incredulously.

"Claimed me?" I ask, confused, I didn't think his words rang true, I should have known better.

"Yes. Just as a wolf can claim their mate, the same can be done for Angels."

"I'm not an Angel," I remind him.

"Doesn't matter. Your boyfriend is part Angel, and now you have a big fat warning sign on you to other Angels," Tanya says before Max can answer.

"How did you learn this?" I ask, my brow furrowed.

"I read a lot when I was at the castle," she replies in a small voice. "She kept me in there for weeks by myself."

I don't know what to say to that, so I turn back to Max. "You and I are going to talk."

He only nods with a smirk attached to those beautifully sinful lips. One that I know I won't care to argue with.

Chapter Sixteen

I'm not really sure what I'm supposed to call Lucifer.

Dad?

Father?

Devil?

Lucifer?

I think I may just stick to Lucifer to be safe.

He stands in front of me, again popping up unannounced, and checks around the small space. I'm currently lying in Max's tent, just having woken up again with Max nowhere in sight.

I sit up, and his eyes zoom in on my neck when I do. My hands go to touch what I know he is looking at.

"You let him mark you?" Lucifer says, his voice

imparting disgust. "A half-breed? You let a half-breed mark you?"

"You forget I am a half-breed too," I remind him.

"You are anything but. *You* are remarkable," he says proudly.

Well shit! I did *not* expect that kind of reaction from him.

I'm not really sure what I should've expected.

I always believed my sisters and I had the same father, yet somehow, I was different, but never put two and two together. I think somewhere in the back of my mind, I knew otherwise, but didn't want to come to terms with whatever that answer might have been.

"Why are you here?" I ask. "Do you plan to just pop in unexpectedly whenever you feel like it?"

He rubs his jaw, considering my question. "No. I guess I'm as drawn to you as I was your mother."

"Eww, that's disgusting."

He pinches the bridge of his nose at my outburst. "Not in that way. Stop that thought, now." The tent flap opens, and Max enters. His tent is the biggest, but having three people in here is somewhat crowded.

"You killed one of my people," Max snarls, his fists clenching at his sides.

"It would be best if you make sure your people don't fuck with my child, then..." Lucifer trails off, but his eyes display the brightest red, and his face is one of pure, unadulterated fury.

Max replies, "Fair enough."

"Fair enough?" I question, incredulous.

"He knows what is important, or he wouldn't have branded you," Lucifer says.

I point to Max. "Branded me? What on this green earth are you doing?"

"You consented."

"You do have to consent," Lucifer adds matter-of-factly.

I cover my face with my hands.

Oh my God.

That was when...

"It's time for me to go," Lucifer says, then disappears.

"It is," Max agrees as he sits next to me and pulls my hands from my face. "You knew you were mine anyway. Now it's cemented."

"What if I choose not to be yours?" I ask, searching his icy-blue gaze.

"That won't happen. I would never do anything intentionally to upset you."

"Lying to me?" I say, eyes wide.

"I didn't lie. I told you when I was fucking you that I needed words, and you gave me your words freely."

I drop backward and pull the sheet up over my head, hiding from him.

"Pretty." I ignore him and just lie there, trying to breathe.

Max lifts the sheet from the bottom and crawls up underneath until his head is level with my breasts, and he's looking up at me. "Are you mad?"

"A little," I answer truthfully.

"Let me help with that," he says as one hand slides up my shirt and palms my breast.

"I'm sure there are more important things you should be doing."

"This world is safer than ours. I've never felt this free in my lifetime." He leans down and kisses my stomach.

"But we aren't free. Don't go underestimating Viper. He has tricks up his sleeve," I tell him.

"Not as many as me." His mouth finds my nipple, and he starts circling it with his tongue before he sucks hard, releasing with a *pop*. I stifle a moan until he repeats the process on the other side.

"I think this is unfair," I tell him.

He stops and meets my eyes. I push him off, and he falls to his side as I sit up. I roll Max onto his back and straddle him, untying his trousers before I pull his large, already hard cock free. It slaps against his stomach, and he puts his hands behind his head, extremely proud as he watches me.

"How, my pretty, is this unfair?"

"You aren't allowed to touch me," I tell him, my expression unmoving. "If you do, I stop, and you aren't allowed to touch me for a week."

"A week?" he asks, with a slow nod. "Not sure you could last that long, but go on... let's see who wins."

I laugh before I grip his cock and begin to stroke. We watch each other, eyes locked onto every move, and he smirks, thinking he will come out the winner.

He very well may, but I hope to prove otherwise.

I squeeze his shaft before I drop my head down and give the tip a kiss. He raises his hips a fraction, then lowers them, so I do it again. But this time, I swirl my tongue around the tip, enticing a groan. My hand doesn't stop moving as I pump up and down and kiss the tip again. Reaching down with my other hand, I grip his balls, and roll them gently, then blow on the tip and pull away. Max groans loudly, and I grin.

"What's the matter?" I ask coyly. Leaning down, I peer at him through my lashes as my tongue darts out and licks his slit, firing him up as he does to me.

Payback.

Such sweet payback.

I will never get sick of this.

He groans, long and low, his hands fisted at his sides—he's so close to grabbing me.

"You will be the death of me," he pants.

"No touching," I warn.

I do it again.

And again.

And again.

Until I know I've pushed him to his limit, and he reaches for me, pulls me up his body, and takes my mouth with his. His hands get busy pulling my pants down, and then he uses his feet to kick them away.

"I said... *no touching*," I whisper against his lips.

"You knew I would fail. With you, I will *always* fail." He kisses me deeply, and I lay my body on top of his, feeling him press against me. I moan into his mouth, and he maneuvers us until I feel him at my entrance. "Fuck."

I feel him slide in, and I sit up slightly as one last tease before sinking all the way down on his shaft. He grips my hips, and before I can move again, he tangles his fingers in my hair and pulls me down, so our lips smash against one another.

"Move," he growls out the word into my mouth.

I try to sit up, but he holds me hostage with his mouth, so I slide up and down his body. The friction against my clit, along with his cock hitting every single right spot, is perfection.

"Max."

"Mmm..." My hips start moving faster and faster, and before I can stop myself, I push off his chest and break our lips apart. My hands find my hair and pull as I ride him hard. Back and forth, back and forth, hitting every amazing position imaginable.

"Fuck, you're beautiful," he whispers, reaching up and massaging my breast. I drop one of my hands to cover his and hold on as I continue riding him.

This is pleasure and seduction all in one.

I can't stop.

I'm not sure I would even if given the opportunity.

"That sweet, sweet pussy is milking the fuck out of my cock," he growls, burying his head into my neck with a kiss that has me whimpering. And before I can come, he flips me, so I land on all fours, slamming right back into me from behind. The orgasm that was building is now intensifying.

"Don't stop."

"Like I could," Max says, smacking my ass. My back arches, and I push back to take him all in. He thrusts in and back until my knees give way as I come with a shuddering scream.

He comes at the same time, pulling out and spilling his cum all over my back as I collapse to the ground. When I turn around, he's holding his cock and shaking it over my back.

"Was that necessary?" I arch a brow.

"Fucking oath. Now, no other fucker will touch what's mine. You smell like me, and that's what I want."

"You were once so well-spoken, and now you are nothing but a dirty talker."

I smile. "Only to you." He leans down and kisses my cheek as I lie there, spent and satisfied. "Don't move. I'll be back to collect you and wash you."

"Is there a lake nearby?" I ask, stifling a yawn.

Who would have thought that my life now would be me getting fucked and sleeping? Growing up, it was about being taught how to fight, and now I'm more worried about when I can see Max again.

I think I may very well be in love with this man.

Once more, I wonder... can you love two men at the same time?

I think I just might.

Though, each love feels uniquely different.

Grim is silent and doesn't take.

Max is happy to take and is far from silent with me.

Each man is opposite to the other, and each holds a spot in my heart.

I don't want to tell Max that, though. He wouldn't like that I still have feelings for Grim. But Grim and I will never go anywhere—it's why it's easier to say nothing.

Max and I—we *will* go places.

I see us lasting a lifetime.

At least, I hope.

I would never have dreamed in a million years I would want to be with someone other than my sisters.

Yet here I am, on my bare stomach as he walks out fully clothed and returns not long after with a blanket.

Max wraps it around me, a towel slung over his shoulder, as he lifts me up and carries me like a baby.

"You have a thing for carrying me." I laugh.

"I have a thing for *you*," is all he replies.

I lean into him as he heads to a lake not far away. No one stops and talks to us. They simply mind their own business.

I smile when I see the crystal-clear water. "It reminds me of your eyes," I tell him as he wades in, not worried about removing his clothes or dropping the blanket. However, he does drop the towel to the ground before submerging us.

"Really?" he asks, brushing my hair off my shoulder and cupping my jaw. "Tell me you'll do something for me."

"What?" I question, staring into those eyes that shine brightly in the moonlight and the reflection of the water.

"Tell me you will never trust your sisters fully or blindly again."

"Why? They are my family."

"You know why. Tatiana loves you. But she loves her children more. It will take time, if it happens at all, for her not to want to lock you away."

"She wouldn't."

"She would," he insists. "I overheard Tanya and Melvon talking. They are here to persuade you to go back in hopes they can convince you to stay with them."

I push away at his words and drop my head under the water.

Why is this my life?

Why did I have to be the chosen one with all this power?

I wish it weren't me.

I wish I were a normal witch falling in love with a normal Angel-demon.

Yet, no matter what I wish, I am not.

I stay under too long for Max's liking, and he pulls me up. Catching my breath, I slick my hair back from my eyes.

"You'll have me. Always me," he says, leaning in and kissing me again.

"I have an idea." He watches me with eager, sparkling eyes. "You should be king."

He laughs. "I am already king... of my people."

"No, I mean of this world. You should be king here."

"Talia." Max reaches out and pulls me behind him. I peer over his shoulder to see a figure standing at the water's edge, holding a towel in her hand.

"I think it's time we talk." I watch as Cinitta's eyes track to Max, then back to me. "Alone."

"That will *not* happen," Max growls.

Cinitta has many gifts, but fire is her strongest. She throws a fireball straight at Max, who catches it and places it into the water as if it's nothing. Her head tilts to the side, and her expression fills with surprise. She studies him for a moment before she turns to face me.

"Viper has the baby," she says before I start wading through the water back to shore.

"Déjà vu," I mutter.

"Huh?" Cinitta asks.

"Oh, you know, just another person in power trying to take something I love."

"He also has the alpha and your sister."

"Fucking hell," I swear, shaking my head.

"Yes, fucking hell." She smiles. "He plans to send you a warning tomorrow at first light. He is thinking possibly your sister's arm."

"Why are you here helping her?" Max asks as he steps onto the bank and reaches for the towel in Cinitta's hand, pulling it from her grasp before wrapping it around my naked body.

"I believe she will be the better option to serve," Cinitta answers him, then looks back to me. "He can't see you anymore. But when you left the wolves, he could see your sister holding the baby and listened. He knows what she is."

"She's a baby," I reply, to which she shakes her head.

"Yes, that may be true, but she is also the daughter of an alpha and a strong witch, and now has the life force inside of her from one of the most powerful people to grace this earth."

"She's right. This can't wait any longer," Max adds, turning to look at Cinitta. "How far is the castle?"

"A few miles that way." She points and looks at me. "You know the way."

I do.

But I had hoped never to walk to that castle again in my life.

Let alone lay my eyes on Viper.

The last time I saw him, he sent me through a damn portal.

Asshole.

Chapter Seventeen

Cinitta leaves us, and we go back to camp, where Max changes clothes, and I watch in fascination as he dresses in all black. His shirt, which has ties on it, slips on easily, as do his leather pants. He pushes his hair back before his eyes lock on mine.

"I'll have you after you are on that throne," he says.

"I don't want the throne," I tell him. "I never have."

He steps forward, brushes my hair back, and starts to dress me. He pulls a shirt similar to his out and slips it over my head, then turns me around so he can do the strings up at the back.

"It's the greatest leaders who never want the power. Those are the leaders who succeed." He kisses my neck before securing the last tie. "Plus, you are mated to a king, which automatically makes you a queen."

"Maybe I can appoint you, and you can do it all." I hear him laugh behind me.

"Yes, sure, whatever it is you want."

I smile before he turns me around. Then my thoughts go to my sister, John, and the baby. How did Viper even manage to get them? John isn't an easy man to capture. I look down as Max drops to the ground and reaches for pants I didn't see before. He slides them up my legs, dressing me as if I am a small child.

"I'm dressing you because you are lost in your head," he answers, as if reading my thoughts. "Your sister will be fine. Call your father if you must." He stands and kisses my head. "He may be a lot of things... *the devil himself*... but I can see the protectiveness he has for you."

"I won't be calling him. We can't trust him. He is a demon, after all."

"He is the king of demons." Max puts both hands on my face, leans in, and kisses my lips. "And you are their princess." He smiles. "As you are my queen." I nod at his words before he lifts a knife I didn't see and pushes it into the back of his trousers. Then holds out a smaller one for me. I take it and slide it into my leather pants and look up at him.

"What if..." A tear leaves my eye.

He wipes it away as if it doesn't belong there.

"You and I are going to sneak in undetected. No one will even know we are coming."

"What about your people? Your guards?"

"They will stay here and protect the camp."

"Okay."

"Are you ready?" he asks and holds out his hand. I place mine in his. "We aren't walking, Talia. You need to take us there. Remember, you know where to go. Just think of somewhere they wouldn't know where to look. Try to remember..."

I close my eyes and *be* where I want to *be*. It's getting easier to move around, and when I open my eyes, we are standing in a room I recognize. It was Veronica's, but it doesn't appear the same.

Actually, it doesn't even get used, by the looks of it. There is dust everywhere, the curtains are hanging at a strange angle, and everything looks unkempt.

"Good. Good girl. Now, where are we?" he asks while checking around.

"The castle," I whisper. "This was Veronica's room."

Max nods and pulls out his knife, holding it close to him.

"If you need to use me, do not hesitate. You know I can handle you taking what you need, so use me whenever required." When I don't answer, he grips my arm and locks eyes with me. "*Talia*, use me."

I nod, unable to form words. The last time I did that here, I ended up killing someone because I got too high on the power. And Max's power is the biggest and best drug there is.

He pushes me behind him as he shuffles toward the door and slowly opens it, glancing back to make sure I'm right behind him. It's late, but that doesn't mean there isn't anything out there. The vampires prefer the night, and Viper... well, who knows what he prefers.

Max nods for me to follow, and I do, staying quiet as possible as we step out. He rounds a corner, and I see the dining hall straight away.

"Where will they be?" Max whispers.

I know where they will be.

Without a shadow of a doubt.

They'll be in *that* room.

I thought it was destroyed, but if Viper's had his way, it would be back in tip-top shape. I nod in the direction of the room, and Max heads that way. He strides forward with power. A power you can practically feel vibrating out of him. When we get to the hallway leading to the room, I pause, unsure if I want to get near it. Max immediately notices, and he turns back to me, kisses me on the lips, nods his head, and turns back around.

How can he be so confident?

I put one foot in front of the other and follow him until we stop at the door.

I hate that door.

I hate everything that it holds.

I hate what it represents.

When I look at that door, all I can think about is Patrick.

I miss him every single day.

I wipe a stray tear away and nod to it. Max pushes the door open, but I stop him from entering. His back goes a little straighter when he peers inside, and then he tenses. I step up to see what he is looking at, spotting Grim with his eyes on Max. It's then I notice he is restrained to the floor with chains holding him immobile.

"Grim!" I gasp, trying to push past Max, but he stops me.

"Don't. It's what Viper wants," Max says.

"But—"

"Maybe I can go in," Max interrupts as he scans the room.

"It traps powers," I tell him, then whisper, "Even mine." He nods, and I can tell he's trying to think of something. Anything. Then he turns his attention back to Grim.

"If I threw you this knife, could you use it?" Max asks him.

Grim glances at his hands and then nods. "If you got it close enough to my hand," Grim replies. Max pulls out a smaller knife, bends down, and, in one swift motion, slides it straight into Grim's hand.

"King Maxilliam."

We both turn to the sound of that voice.

Standing behind us is Alan, the seer who helped me with my power when we opened the portal.

"Alan?" Max says, clearly confused.

He isn't wearing his normal clothes, instead he is dressed as a king. He steps forward and, before we know what he's doing, he kicks Max into the room. I'm so shocked by what is happening that I don't try to stop him when he reaches for me. My head goes dizzy at the contact, and I can't stand straight. I wobble, and Alan pushes me to the ground. Then he pulls my hands behind my back and ties them tightly. My head is hurting, and I don't understand what is happening.

"I thought this would be harder." Alan tsks and looks into the room. I turn my head on the floor, and when I do, I see that Grim and Max are both free. Alan places his hand on the side of the door, and when Max charges toward it, he hits an invisible barrier. I see it waver when he collides.

"Alan, think about what you are doing."

"I did, sir. I am serving the rightful king."

"And who is that?"

"My son, of course." I can hear the smile in his voice as other footsteps come our way. I'm lifted from the floor, and when I look up, Viper approaches, wearing a green cape and a broad smile on his lips.

"I guess it wasn't a bad thing, after all, sending you to that place. You did bring my father back. And for that, I won't kill your sister. The wolf, on the other hand..." He taps his jaw. "... I'm still undecided." I glance through the door at Grim and Max, who are both staring at me. "I didn't plan to capture him, but I won't lie and say I've never wondered what it was like to be Death." Viper turns to face him. "Tell me. If I killed her right now, how would you collect her soul? Would it just float away and never be seen again?" Viper asks.

He turns back to me when his taunt gets no reply. "Everyone that saves you is here, child. Now it's time we go and talk." Two guards grab onto my arms, dragging me away, and I hear Max call out my name. I can't move my hands and feet. They won't cooperate, and I don't know why.

We reach a large sitting area, and as my eyes take in

the room, I see a cage set up in the middle. And behind that is another cage. In the first one is John, who seems to be knocked out, but in the second one is my sister and her baby.

"Talia," Tatiana says in surprise. "You shouldn't have come." She shakes her head and holds her baby even tighter. "You shouldn't have come," she reiterates, her hands trembling against her newborn.

"I had to," I whisper. My eyes locked on hers, she is looking at me with confusion as she holds her baby in her hands tightly.

"Yes, yes, of course, you had to. That's what you girls are known for," Viper says with an eye roll as I'm jerked to a stop and forced to the floor.

"Thanks to my father, I was able to come up with a potion to subdue your powers," Viper tells me with a smile. "Probably not best to let strangers help you with your powers, Talia."

"Thanks, I'll take that into consideration in the future," I snap.

Cinitta walks in, and her eyes find mine as I lie on the floor. She looks away quickly before Viper notices and heads over to him.

"You should have stayed in that other world. It would have been better for you than your fate here." I try to move, but I can't. I try to draw from my powers, and I feel them lurking just under the surface, but it's

187

like they're stuck and unable to move forward. "Cinitta is going to watch you, so be on your best behavior and stay quiet while I go and speak to a certain Angel of Death." Viper turns and strides out, his father going with him. When I see he is gone, I search for Cinitta and find she is standing off near the cages, her gaze firmly fixed on the floor.

"Why do you serve him?" I ask.

"You know why," she answers.

"Sometimes people who we thought were heroes change. He has changed, Cinitta." She doesn't reply.

I check on John, who's still knocked out. "What did they do to him?" I ask.

Cinitta looks at John's cage.

"A wolf isn't meant to be caged. They go insane and will tear it to shreds. This cage is strong enough to withhold most wolves, but Viper is not sure about this one. He is the alpha, after all, so he thought it safer to knock him out."

"He'll wake soon," my sister says, her baby clutched in her arms. She locks eyes with me. "And so will you. Remember who you are, Talia. You aren't someone who can be broken like this." I want to believe her, but I don't know how. I literally feel stuck, and my powers don't feel the same.

A part of me is missing.

And I don't like the feeling at all.

"Cinitta, help me."

"The last time I did that..." She turns toward me, and I watch as a tear leaves her eye.

"What?"

She quickly wipes her cheek.

"I lost a sister."

I gasp at her words. "I didn't have a choice," I choke out.

She shakes her head. "I'm not talking about then... after."

"Oh." I attempt to move, but it's hard. Everything feels so heavy.

But then I hear my name.

It's loud and filled with power.

Max is angry.

Chapter Eighteen

"Talia," Tatiana calls my name. "Think about it. Whatever they are using on you is created with power. What do you do with power?" she says in a whisper. "You take it."

My head rests on the floor, and I hear the screams of Max, my name constantly leaving his lips. I try to do as my sister says, but nothing happens. And then John starts to stir. It's quiet at first, but I see his slight movements through the cage bars. My sister notices as well.

"Talia, you have to do something. John won't be able to handle being in a cage." I watch him as his body comes around. I still can't work out how to move, though.

It's draining.

I'm exhausted.

The fatigue is making me want to close my eyes.

My sister keeps on calling my name, but I just can't seem to care.

Why do I keep ending up in these situations?

A loud bang rings through the room, followed by a growl so deep that it makes me lift my head.

John is awake.

His body slams into the sides of the cage, but it's not moving. He turns into his wolf and continues throwing himself against the bars.

"Cinitta, let them go."

Cinitta looks down at me, her purple hair bright as she stands in the light near the cages.

"Viper won't know. Let them go and blame me."

"He *will* know," she says. "I can't risk my life again."

John's growls grow incessantly louder as he remains trapped in the cage.

"John, stop! You're scaring the baby." Tatiana tries to calm him down. "John, look, we are both fine. We're fine." He pauses for only a moment before he starts again. Tatiana's head drops in defeat as John's growls only become louder and louder with each minute that passes.

Then we hear a bang.

Cinitta whips her head to the doors.

"Cinitta, what's that?"

She steps away from us, and I try to reach her, but she isn't close enough.

"I don't know. It sounds like it's coming from the front doors," she says, just as the sound of another explosion reaches us. Her gold eyes find mine, and worry covers her face.

John thrashes in his cage, back and forth, growling so loudly and viciously that I want to cover my ears, but I feel so tired.

So, so tired.

Alan enters the room. His eyes find mine and then Cinitta's before they flick to the door as another explosion echoes through the room.

"Carry her and leave them," Alan commands before turning back to head the same way as he came.

Cinitta reaches for me and lifts me with ease. I manage to look back to see my sister watching John as he tries with everything he can to get through that cage, but nothing he does helps the situation.

I feel us cross through a barrier before the front doors are torn open and wolves flood in, heading straight toward the cages. One transforms back into human form and manages to unlock John's cage. John jumps free, his howl reverberating off the walls as he turns to my sister and breaks through her cage with little effort. As soon as she and the baby are free, my sister stands and leans down, her face burying in his fur. He lets out a soft huff as she touches his snout, then she kisses his head, and he shifts back. Her free arm wraps around his waist as she kisses him deeply.

One of the wolves approaches Cinitta and me. The minute she reaches us, I can see the barrier and know the wolf does as well. She puts up her hand to test it, and when she does, she yelps so loudly it pains my ears. When I look at her hand, I see half of it has been singed.

"Yes, neat little trick, wouldn't you say?" Viper steps forward, bends down, and leans into my ear. "Not even they are stupid enough to try to get through." I watch as my sister shifts toward us, the baby now safely tucked in John's arms. She sees the barrier and looks at the wolf who attempted to touch it before she looks back at me.

Tatiana closes her eyes and starts to hum. She does this for a few seconds, and everyone just watches and waits to see what will happen. But it's not that easy. Viper has a strong spell in place, probably created with the help of demons.

"You tried," Viper taunts and walks off.

Tatiana stares at me helplessly as John steps up next to her. He whispers something in her ear, and she nods before looking back at me.

"We have to go to our daughter," she quietly says, sadness lacing her voice.

There was a time when she would never have dreamed of leaving me. It's funny how situations change, how people change, really. We are no longer the same girls who grew up in that small house. She has her own family now, while I am still trying to work out my life. I'm a little jealous of the person she is and what she has, but I'm also thankful she now has what she's always deserved. Tatiana was made to be a mother.

It seems I am made for the complete opposite.

Max screams my name again, and I feel so helpless without him by my side. Alan grabs my arm and pulls me back toward the door, diverting my attention for what feels like just a second. But when I glance at where my sister was standing, I see that she and all the wolves have now left.

Will they come back for me? I'm not sure I should rely on them for help. I need to work out how to get out of here on my own.

Cinitta stands by as I'm dropped unceremoniously to the floor in front of the room where Max and Grim are being held. Max is at the door, drops to his knees, and then tries to reach me, but he can't because of the invisible barrier. I see the stress coating his face, and mine would match if I felt more like myself. He isn't used to not being in charge or having a way out of something. After all, he is a powerful Angel-demon and is used to having everything go his way.

"Are you okay?" he asks, desperate concern lacing his tone and making me want to cry.

Viper smiles down at me, answering before I can. "She is fine. Still breathing, as you can see..." He pauses just to be an ass. "For now."

Over Max's shoulder, I see Grim sitting against the wall, elbows on his knees and head dropped down low. *What is he thinking?*

"Grim?" I say his name, and he lifts his eyes. Those silver eyes that always search my face are now lost. He doesn't know what to do, and he always does, apart from when it comes to me.

"So, you move for her," Viper comments. "Well, maybe now you *will* listen." Viper leans down and lifts my head as if I'm a ragdoll, and out of nowhere, I feel a knife at my throat. Grim shoots to his feet, and in the next second, he is at the door right next to Max. He locks eyes with me.

"This isn't how you die," he promises me.

"But it could be how she suffers," Viper says, and I feel the blade dig in a little deeper.

"Fucking let her go," Max shouts.

"Tell your friend to give me what I want," Viper says.

What the hell? I have no idea what they're talking about.

"I can't," Grim says as he stares at me. "I can't."

Viper presses the blade a little harder against my neck, and blood wells with the sting until it drips on the floor.

Grim looks away.

Max is still shouting, only now with more vigor.

And the next thing I know... I'm gone.

There is no longer a knife at my neck, and I'm not on the floor looking up at the only two men in my life that have ever meant everything to me.

I'm surrounded by blackness. *Is this death? Did he manage to kill me? I just don't know.*

I move my arms, and a small sigh leaves me at the realization that I am once again in control of my body.

Managing to stand, I check around the all-black room. I can't see where it starts or where it ends. It's as if the room is a circle.

"Talia." I recognize the voice straight away. Turning around, Lucifer is standing there. He steps closer and runs a finger over my neck. It's then I realize the wound is healed.

"You let another bleed you?" he says, shaking his head.

"I didn't let him."

"Another is not permitted to have our blood, let alone bleed us."

"I couldn't move," I argue.

"But you could, could you not?" he asks, his head

dropping to the side as he watches me. "You are still alive, after all."

"I'm alive?" I ask, looking around.

"Yes, my dear, this is not Hell. I'm not sure you are ready for that yet."

"He drugged me," I tell him.

"With something made here. Now, tell me, daughter, whose child are you?" He lays his hand on my shoulder. "Stop letting it hold you back, and start using that knowledge to fight." My hand goes to my neck, and Lucifer nods. "Because if you don't, I will. And you will not like the outcome if I have to come." His red eyes shine brightly before he disappears.

When I blink again, I'm standing on the other side of the barrier that burned the wolf.

I look up to see a confused Viper—*yeah, that makes two of us*. He takes something from Alan. It looks like a gun, which he shoots through the barrier at the door and hits Max with. Max pulls out a needle and lets it drop to the floor. I watch in shock as he becomes weaker and stumbles to the side. Viper removes the barrier that was holding him inside, and Max falls through the doorway. Grim takes the opportunity to step out and disappear. The barrier that is holding me back is still in place, and Viper starts swearing and cursing at me because Grim has gotten away.

"Call him back." He lifts Max's head from the floor and places the same blade that is coated with my blood against his neck. "Call him back, or I'll slice his throat."

"Why?" I ask. My eyes locked on Max, if he hurts him...

Max's eyes close, and I see him fighting to stay awake.

"I want my family back. It's what I've always wanted. The Angel of Death can do that," he screams. "Now... call. Him. Back."

"No." I touch the barrier and expect it to burn me, but it doesn't. My hand goes straight through it. I smile as I realize I can step through, and it won't hurt me.

Viper appears as shocked as I feel, his white eyes wide and his father shaking his head at me.

"He won't come back," I tell Viper. He smiles.

"If I'm going to die, do you really think I will make it easy?" he states, confusing me.

Alan runs at me, and I lift my hand and reach for him but he pushes a needle into my skin, I shake it off fast before my hand touches him, I start draining his power. And I keep draining until I feel every bit of his power leave his body. He drops to the floor at my feet, and his head hits hard, knocking him out cold. The rush hits me immediately, but I can't stop.

I need Max.

As I start toward him, Viper smiles.

And in the next instant, the very same knife that made me bleed slices through Max's neck.

Shock hits me first.

Did he just...

He did.

Max drops to the floor face-first into a pool of his blood. I watch for a moment as it grows bigger, then I turn my gaze on Viper.

Does he think he will get out of this alive for hurting someone I love, not just someone, my Max. That is unacceptable. In more ways then one.

"You are the Devil's daughter," he says, eyes wide. I catch my reflection and see that my eyes are glowing red. I can't move, but I know what I want. I want my hands around Viper's neck, want to feel the life leave him. I summon him closer, and he is pulled by a force so strong that not even he himself can stop it. The second his neck is in my hands, I smile.

"I'm going to enjoy this," I seethe.

My head lolls back as I feel his power crawling all over me like snakes finding their home.

Oh, to see what he has seen.

He is the most powerful seer of this generation. It explains how he survived when no one else has.

I see myself in the future, sitting on a throne, dressed in all black.

And as I get to the person sitting next to me, I snap his neck.

And I enjoy every second of it, to how his body falls to the floor, lifeless now. No evidence of life left thanks to me.

Chapter Nineteen

Not caring, I let him fall to the floor in a heap and step over him. I rush to Max, who is lying lifeless in a pool of his own blood.

My heart cracks. Even through the high, it hurts with a force I'm not used to bearing. I drop to my knees, not caring that they are now covered in blood. *Max's blood*.

My hands touch him and I try, I try as hard as I can to heal him, but I'm coming up blank. Why is it blank? I push harder, my head hurts, my body hurts, but most of all, my heart hurts. Tears start clogging my eyes, why are they doing that, I can bring him back, the same way I brought my niece back. But why isn't it working.

The needle.

My eyes close again, heavier, from the drug or from

the pain, which I am not sure. I run my hands through his hair and smile at the thought that he kissed me the last time I did this. Then, my vision becomes blurry, and I realize it's because of the tears continuously falling from my eyes.

This isn't fair.

How could this happen?

How did I let this happen?

And why wasn't I smart enough to stop it?

Bodies surround me, but there's only one that I care about. I want to breathe life into him, to tell him to wake up. Even though I know it's not possible, I try anyway.

I grab at his clothes—the very same ones that we've torn off together.

I hate that I love him.

I hate that he put me in this position that now, not only did I manage to fall in love with someone I thought I could spend the rest of my life with, he should've known. He should've known that he would leave me like this and that this would destroy me. That even though I hear another breath come close to me— one that very well could belong to someone who could snap my neck—I pay no attention because the breath and the heartbeat I want to hear no longer exists.

That heart no longer beats.

And it will no longer love me.

That realization hurts more than words can describe.

"Talia."

I know someone is saying my name, but my head just doesn't want to lift from its spot on Max's back to see who it is.

"Talia."

I reach for something, but I'm not even sure what it is until it surrounds me. I put us in a cocoon that protects us both.

I can no longer hear my name being called, and I don't want to look around to see the destruction that surrounds us. That will only remind me of his death.

Why couldn't I stop it?

Why?

I curl myself up into a ball and slide my hands up his torso.

If I could breathe life into him, I would.

If I could give him my life, I would.

I hear knocking.

But I pay no attention.

I start to drift off.

And as I do, I hear his voice calling me.

"She doesn't want to be disturbed."

I hear someone say.

"And who are you, her slave?"

I know that voice.

"Leave her be."

"I will do no such thing. You leave."

"No, she needs protection. And since no one else seems to want to do that, I will."

"You think you should be the one protecting her?" I hear a laugh. "Like you protected and served Viper?"

"Viper is no longer living and no longer holds anything over me."

"So why do you want to serve her?"

"Because she is a queen. We all know it."

I open my eyes to see Cinitta and Tanya arguing.

"Shut up!" I scream.

My hands are still under Max's shirt, but his body is no longer warm. "Max. Max, wake up." I push him, but he doesn't move. "Max, please wake up," I try again. He still doesn't move.

I thought it was a dream, a nightmare. I had hoped and prayed it was. But as my hands hold his body and feel the coldness when he usually feels so warm, I know we're not that fortunate.

It's my reality.

My nightmare.

And I hate it.

I hate this whole fucking world right now. I want to burn it to the ground along with every fucker living in it.

I feel myself becoming so angry that I just can't stop myself. Before I know it, the castle is on fire, and my sister starts screaming at me to move. But I don't have the will to move. I can't seem to leave Max, even if I wanted to.

Cinitta tries to reach for me.

But with a single movement of my hand, she is gone.

"Do we plan to burn the world down as well?" I turn my head to see my father standing there. He's dressed in a red suit, which is fitting, really. He looks around and leans down to me. "You need to stop this."

"Stop what?"

"You are opening worlds and destroying this one."

"I'm not. Fuck off." He places a hand on Max, and then Max is gone. Along with all his blood.

I fall to the ground, my hands searching desperately for him.

"What did you do? Where is he?"

"Stop what you are doing."

I turn and get in his face. "Where is he?" I scream. "What did you do with him?"

He takes a deep breath and touches my shoulder. "Calm down."

"No. Where is he?" I say through gritted teeth.

The castle starts to crumble around us. But, apart from Viper's body and his father's, no one else is in here.

"You need to calm down."

"Stop telling me to calm down. Bring. Him. Back."

My father sighs, then I feel us moving, and the smell of sulfur reaches my nose.

"Why did you bring her here?"

I turn to see Valefar, shirtless, his body marked with black lines, standing on ground that is red in color. When I glance down, I know I am somewhere I don't recognize. When I look at Lucifer, he is now shirtless as well, and wings sprout out from his back.

Looking away from him, I see red hills, red dirt.

Where am I?

"Where am I?" I voice the question raised in my mind as I step away from both of them and toward a fire.

"You are in Hell." I pause as I near the fire and look back to Lucifer. "You are beautiful with wings," I tell him. "Now, take me back."

"No, you need to calm down."

"And you think being here will calm me down?" I yell at him.

"Shit! What have you done to her?" Valefar asks.

"The seer killed her lover," Lucifer declares.

At his words, I feel myself snap just a little more. The ground beneath me starts to shake and Lucifer walks up to me, grabs my arm, and pulls me to him.

"Stop, right now." When I glance at his eyes, I see the Devil, which is only fitting.

Lucifer growls, and as I go to speak, something hits me in the back of my head so I fall forward. Lucifer catches me, and my hands brush his wings. "You hit her?"

"Would you prefer I killed her?" Valefar says from behind me. Lucifer shakes his head. "What, you want her to bring Hell into the world?"

"Of course, I don't."

"Well, if that was me, you would have killed me," Valefar argues.

"You want me to kill her?" Lucifer asks incredulously.

My head feels dizzy as I push away from Lucifer.

"Well, she is causing a lot of trouble."

"She is going to be queen. Wouldn't you rather someone like her ruling that world?"

"No, *I* would rather rule."

"You will never rule, Valefar."

"You are a real asshole. You know that, right?"

My hands go to the back of my head, and I rub it.

"It's time you go back," Lucifer says. "Don't destroy the world in the process." He touches my forehead, and I'm standing outside of the castle as it falls to the ground.

Something that was once untouchable, sacrosanct, is now falling to pieces as if it had been nothing but rubble all along.

"Talia." Cinitta reaches me, and I turn to her. "Are you okay?"

"I'm going to destroy anyone who served him," I tell her. Fire bubbling up in me.

"Where do you want to start?" Cinitta asks.

"Talia, you need to go and see Tatiana." I ignore Tanya as she comes closer. "Talia." Her hand touches my arm, and I shrug it off. "Talia, Max would want you with your family."

"What did you say?" I spin to face her, stepping up close.

"Max would want you with family."

"Max is dead, Tanya, so leave his name from your mouth!" I scream.

Melvon is there, and he reaches for Tanya, pulling her away from me.

"Scared, Melvon?" I ask him, laughing. "You should be. Did I tell you who my daddy is?" I sneer. "Let me ask you, who is yours? Because I'm about to destroy every last vampire, so make sure you aren't around when I do it, Melvon."

"Talia, you wouldn't," Tanya says, shocked.

"I will." Cinitta follows me as I leave. "They are all going to fucking die!"

Chapter Twenty
TANYA

The fairy with purple hair follows my sister. I just stand there and watch as they walk off.

Does Talia realize what she is doing?

She can't destroy a whole race.

That's what the queen did with the seers, and look where that got us. I go to follow her, to tell her that's crazy, but Melvon pulls me back.

"She can't," I plead. "I have to stop her."

"Did you see her?" he asks, standing in front of me and blocking my path. "Really see her? That is not your sister right now. That's a woman pained beyond repair. She wants revenge. And revenge is what she will get. And you will not stop her because I can't risk your life." His last words make me pause. I stare at him and shake my head. My sister would never hurt me, not in this lifetime and definitely not in the next.

"She would never hurt me."

"She may not, but she's done something to our world already. I can feel it changing." I understand what he is saying. I may not be as powerful as either one of my sisters, but I know that something in the air has changed, and it's not for the better.

"We need to get back home to tell John and your sister what happened." Melvon leans in and kisses my lips. It's soft and tender, everything he is for me. "Don't worry, okay?" He brushes my hair behind my ears before we turn and start our trek back to the wolves.

Straight away, I spot Tatiana.

She sits on the grass, her baby asleep next to her, watching her other little one play. I walk over and pick the baby up, cuddling her and keeping her close to my chest as my sister studies me.

"What happened?" she asks.

There was a time when she wouldn't have had to ask those questions because she would've been there. She was the most protective of Talia. But things change, loves change, and I'm not sure how to tell her what happened. "You weren't able to bring her back?" she asks. "What of Viper?"

"He's dead," I tell her. "She did it."

"Good, I'm glad."

"The castle has been razed to the ground." She perks up at that, and her eyes fall on her baby in my arms.

"Did she do that as well?"

"Yes."

"Shit. She's angry."

"She is." Like I have never seen before. "And there is something else."

"What?"

"Max is dead." She freezes, doesn't even blink, and stays like that for a good minute before finally asking, "Where is she?"

"Off to kill all the vampires. Anyone who served Viper is going to die," I tell her. "I've never seen her like this."

"She wouldn't," Tatiana whispers.

"Oh, but she would."

"Get the babies!" John shouts as he rushes over to us. He scoops the baby from my arms.

"What? What's wrong?" Tatiana stands, checking around, confused.

"Grab what you can and run," he says, sounding panicked, reaching for his mate and pulling her to him as Melvon approaches with their other child.

"What's happening?" I ask as soon as he reaches us.

Twenty or so wolves start in our direction, and I see something behind them.

Is that?

No.

It couldn't be.

"Mother?" I say, confused.

"Don't look, just run," John urges.

Melvon reaches for my hand as what appears to be my mother reaches a wolf. She touches him, and I watch in horror as he drops to the ground, the life gone from him in an instant.

"What is that?" Melvon tugs on my hand as I stand frozen at the sight before me.

"They are called yorks. It's just one, but they are powerful," a wolf says. "You can't let it touch you. If you do, it will take your soul."

"So... run, Tanya."

I do as he says and start running with them. I check over my shoulder and watch it touch another, then drain everything it once was and now is never going to be.

"How did this happen?" John asks the wolf who told us what it was—he is from Max's world.

"A portal is the only way."

"Who is strong enough to open a portal?" John asks.

He looks to Tatiana.

"Your sister."

"No, she wouldn't. Does she know those things were there?" Tatiana asks.

"She does. King Maxilliam showed them to her."

"It's a mistake," Tatiana says, but keeps on running.

We all follow, not stopping until we finally get to the forest. Since Viper has left the forest, it's not the same as it once was—it was full of tricks and games that kept anyone away. Now it's once again a simple forest one can get lost in amongst the trees and under-growth. John has run through it many times and knows the way out. We all follow, ignoring how tired we are. We can't stop because if we do, we could end up exactly the same as the others who have managed to get close to the york.

We don't know how fast they travel or even how to kill them.

We just know we can't stand around and wait for the inevitable.

As night falls and our feet start to bleed, we reach the end of the forest. And what lies in front of us is absolute destruction. There is no other word for it. We've exited the forest where Max's people once were living. They lie on the ground, blood everywhere. Lives shattered with hardly anyone left.

Melvon moves forward and sniffs around. He can

smell the difference between life and death—I guess it's one of the perks of being a vampire. When he gets to a woman on the ground, he hovers over her and cuts his wrist. He leans down and pours his blood into her mouth. It doesn't take long before she can start moving again. Then she sits up and screams when she sees him.

"What happened?" Tatiana asks the woman.

"The vampires. They attacked." Her eyes well with tears as she looks at Melvon. "I don't want to be like you."

"You won't be," he says, stepping back to me.

"King Maxilliam is always here to protect us, but we don't know where he is."

"He's dead," one of the wolves informs her.

The older lady nods her head and reaches for a knife. She offers us a sad smile. "I don't want to live in a world where he isn't in it. No one will ever protect us the way King Maxilliam did." She slices her own throat, and Melvon moves quickly to grab her, so she doesn't slam her head on the ground.

"I'm sorry," Melvon whispers.

The lady only offers a small smile before she stops breathing.

I watch as he places her down ever so carefully. He closes her eyes so she can no longer see the world that she died in. Hopefully, wherever she goes next is a place where death isn't always upon us, where there is peace and tranquility.

We should know of places like this—we are supernatural, after all—but all we know is that Heaven and Hell exist. And we're fighting for our rightful place, but sometimes we get confused about which plane is the right one, just as my sister is right now. She isn't aware that what she's doing, or what she might do, is going to land her in Hell. But maybe that's where she wants to be—she is a daughter of the King of Hell.

I know her better than that, though.

Despite everything that has just happened, she is a good person, and no amount of pain will change that. I hope.

"Do you think she has reached them yet?" I ask Melvon.

"Reached who?" John asks.

"Talia was going after the vampires."

"Why?"

I don't answer, so he turns to Melvon. "Why, Melvon?"

"To kill them all," he states.

John is shocked by this news. He scratches his jaw before he turns to his wolves. "So, she's opened a portal, and now she is off to destroy an entire race?" he asks. He stalks over to Tatiana and says, "I can't let her do this. I may hate their kind, but she has no right to do that."

"You won't be able to stop her," I tell him.

Tatiana and I meet eyes, and I know she agrees.

"I may not be able to kill her"—he looks at their baby, knowing they are linked—"but I will stop her." He walks off, and most follow him, apart from us. Melvon wraps an arm around me and holds me close.

"We will camp here tonight!" John yells. "Clear the dead, bury them, and set up watches. We don't want those things coming back."

"I won't touch the dead," I tell Melvon, and he kisses my head.

"You won't have to. I will do it. Go... help your sister."

I watch as he starts lifting bodies, carrying them into the forest. I can't remember how I fell in love with him because it was slow and fast all at the same time. But I remember the first night he entered my bed and the first time we touched.

I was scared to touch him—he's a vampire, after all.

I had never been with a man before, either. I wasn't like my sisters, who were experienced in many ways. I'd always kept to myself and was quiet, preferring it that way.

"Do you think she knows what she is doing?"

217

Tatiana asks, breaking me from my thoughts. I sit down with her and smile at the baby. I'm surprised she's asking me this question because, usually, Tatiana is so sure of everything.

"Yes, she is aware. And she's in pain."

"I was in pain when I thought I lost her..." She pauses, her face pinching with distress. "I didn't try to destroy a whole race, though."

"But you would have if you had the power," I state.

She stays quiet, and we sit there as the moon rises and the stars begin to shine.

Melvon comes over and kisses my cheek before he reaches down and picks me up. I turn in his embrace and wrap my legs around him as he carries me off.

"I washed in the stream, so I shouldn't have any blood on me," he tells me. I nod and lay my head on his chest as he walks us into a small tent just big enough for us both to fit inside.

"I'm worried for this world."

Melvon doesn't reply as I reach for him and pull his shirt from his body. I then remove my own, putting my breasts on full display. He pulls me to him until I'm straddling his lap.

"I hope to never be worried for us. You are the only sure thing in my life," I tell him as I tilt my head, offering him my neck. Melvon kisses it softly before I feel his teeth sink in. He drinks slowly as my body starts to move against him. I get high from the pleasure I give him. His hands wander, tugging at my pants as he pulls the blood from my veins. When he's had his fill, I shift away, and he licks his lips, his fangs retracting.

"You never have to be worried for us." He quickly flips me until I'm lying below him. Melvon pulls his hard cock free and pushes my legs open, his finger finding my entrance. "I live for you now." He kisses the top of my pussy before he licks between the folds. His tongue slides up and down, circling my wetness before he stops, and I feel his fangs enter my upper thigh. At the same time, he slides two fingers inside and begins to pleasure me endlessly.

I reach for him, and he stops tasting me, knowing I need more of him. Licking over the wound, he crawls up my body, and his cock slips between my legs, teasing me.

"You'll never leave me?" I ask him as he slides inside, our matching moans filling the space around us.

His mouth finds mine. "Never."

Chapter Twenty-One

TALIA

They say to take a life is a sin.

I have come to realize I am turning more and more into a sinner.

I stand there, a cold smile on my lips, watching as a vampire walks out of its flashy home. The type of home they never deserved but always had. They always thought they were better than us witches.

Why? I'm not really sure.

They aren't more powerful.

They may have strength on their side, sure.

But definitely not power.

No, that sits with us.

It sits with me.

"Should we?" Cinitta nods to the vampire. She isn't her usual fairy self—she is back to what she was when I first met her. Fire engulfs her scale-covered body, making her stronger this way.

I often wondered how vampires became the more dominant species, but then I remember the Angels... and Veronica. That all seems like so long ago now.

"Talia." I turn to Bronik. "What are you doing?" he asks.

"Fancy seeing you here. It's been a long time."

"Talia, why are you here?"

I reach for my power. When I feel it, I smile as I fling it at him, sticking him to where he stands. His mouth opens wide in shock, but words don't leave it. The vampire that was on his way to probably kill us pauses when he sees the Angel. He takes one look at me and is gone, back into his fancy house.

"See what you did? You scared my fun away." I pout at Bronik, shaking my head. "That's not really nice of you now, is it?" I wave my hand and unfreeze him.

He stumbles, but quickly rights himself. "How did you do that?" he asks, looking around. "And why are you covered in blackness?" I glance down at myself.

"What blackness?"

"It pours from you. It's eating away at you." He steps forward, and I look to the ground and halt him from coming any closer to me.

"You can stay and watch the show if you'd like," I offer. "Did you know all my life we were slaves to them?" I point to the house. "I hated them. How could we let them dominate us when I knew I was stronger than them?"

"You are indeed stronger," Bronik agrees.

"I know. But not strong enough to not get trapped... not once but twice," I say, shaking my head. "Did you know my father before he was the King of Hell?" I ask Bronik. He only nods. "What about Grim? Did he know him?"

"Yes, the Angel of Death and the King of Hell are old friends, Talia."

Yeah, I gathered as much.

"I've been contemplating how I will kill all the vampires. Sitting in that house, they are probably forming a plan." I glance back to Cinitta. "Fire, maybe?" I ask Bronik. "That kills a vampire, right?"

"It does," he confirms.

"What about loss of power?" I smile. "Do you think that from here, I could take their power?"

"No, you have to be touching them."

"They are connected, though, right? What if I got the one who made them all and took his power? Would that then destroy them?"

Bronik is quiet for a long time before he decides it's probably best not to answer me.

"That's okay, fire it is." I reach back and offer Cinitta my hand. Through her fire, she grips mine, and I take some of her power. She falters just a bit as I feel it leaving her body and coming to me. I suck it until a large fireball is formed in front of me. It's so large it lights up the whole area, and you would think it's daytime.

I lock eyes with Bronik. "They said to rule, I had to be cruel. I didn't believe them. But I do now." I let the fireball go at the same time I release Cinitta's arm. The burning orb flies through house after house, incinerating them. When it finally hits the last house, it evaporates, and I grin in the light of the inferno in front of us.

All these beautiful houses that once were admired from afar are now being burned to the ground.

"You don't have to be cruel," Bronik says.

"Yes, I do. Otherwise, what happened will continue to happen," I say as vampires leave their nests and gather in a group. All eyes lock on me, and I wave a hand, setting Bronik free.

He leaves without saying goodbye.

Asshole.

I turn around to speak to Cinitta and stare in surprise as Bronik reappears, wraps his arms around her, and disappears again.

That's okay. I didn't need them in order to destroy the vampires anyway.

The first vampire walks up to me, thinking he has a chance.

He doesn't.

He sneers.

His clothes smell like fire, and I can't help but smirk.

"Witch," he seethes. "You will pay with your life. But first..." I let him get so close that his fangs touch my neck, but not enough to drink, just graze, before I freeze him. Then I pull away and get close to his ear. "Vampire, you will be first." My hand lands on his chest, and I suck the powerful energy he has right from his body. He turns to ash as he dies on the ground.

And the high that fills me is so, so beautiful.

I start walking and see myself as if I am looking down from above.

My hair is wild and free. My eyes are so red I think they have the appearance of blood.

Vampire after vampire comes straight for me, and I take each one down as they do.

I wonder what our world would be like without the vampires.

Maybe they should be extinct? They are dead, after all, so it's only fair they go and meet their maker.

"Witch." The word is hissed over and over again at me.

And then, my brother stands in front of me.

"Talia." He says my name instead of my nickname.

"Did you come to join me?" I ask him, grinning.

"I think you've had your fun," he says, taking in the scene in front of him. There are piles of ash everywhere, some vampires hiding behind burned rubble, while others are trying to kill me.

They won't be able to.

No matter how fast they are, it's their only skill, and I am faster, stronger.

I have many skills, and I am happy to show each and every one of them right here and right now.

"We need the scum in this world, Wings. We need them to feed us."

"I'm sure some will be left," I say as one comes up behind me. He almost gets to me. *Almost.* I spin quickly, grip his neck, and start sucking from him. What I didn't expect was for him to have a knife, which he plunges straight into my stomach.

Vampires hardly use weapons—they think of themselves as too strong, too almighty to need them.

He turns to ash as I step back. I pull the knife from my stomach and turn to face Valefar.

"This will make them crazy. My blood, that is." I

look at the knife and see it's not just an ordinary knife. It's the Angel knife.

Ha, he thought I was an Angel.

And I thought no one could use this knife.

"Bronik!" I scream for him, and it doesn't take long before he appears, dropping Cinitta to the ground at my feet. She is still tired from when I took her power. "Why did you take her?"

He glances down at my wound. "You are bleeding."

"I am. Now, why did you take her?" I ask again.

"You need to stop siphoning." He glances at Cinitta. "She is strong, this one."

"I know, but you are a real dick, you know that?" He smiles his knowing, cocky smile. Cinitta goes to speak, but before she can utter a word, I rush Bronik and slam the knife into his chest. He steps back, his eyes going wide, clearly not expecting that.

I once thought of him as handsome.

Now all I see is a broken Angel.

I pull the knife free, and he shakes his head in disappointment.

"I forgive you," he says before he vanishes with feathers floating to the ground in his wake.

"Oh shit. Daddy is going to be pissed with you." Valefar cackles behind me. I turn to him, and he takes the knife from me. "Just so you don't think of using this on our father. We can't have that now, can we." He winks before he, too, is gone.

"Talia." I turn to Cinitta. "I think it's time we rest." Her eyes are heavy, so I reach for her, and her long purple hair cascades around both of us as I help her up. "You killed him," she whispers. "An Angel."

"I'm sure he deserved it," I tell her. "Now, close your eyes. We are going somewhere." She does as I say, and I transport us to the small town where I grew up. I look at my old house in front of me and smile. Some of it has been repaired to what it used to be, the rest is a work in progress.

Francis steps out of her house next door and looks to Cinitta, who stands on shaky legs.

"You're home," she says, making her way to us. "And you brought a fire witch." She reaches for Cinitta, who takes her hand, and helps her walk. "We fixed your house." Other witches appear as I push the small gate open. Francis and Cinitta follow me through.

This place holds memories of good times.

Of how my sisters and I would play late at night before our mother would call us to come inside.

Of where I learned to fight and hide my magic as well as use it.

I push the front door open and note it is not the same inside. Even though the colors are there, it's not how I remember it. Gone are the old walls that more than likely contained mold, and in their place are new planks that smell of fresh pine.

"We hoped you would reside back here where you belong, as our queen," Francis says. I turn around to see Cinitta sitting on the floor, her head between her legs as she takes deep breaths. I walk over and place my hand on her head, giving her some of her power back. I don't need it now, as I'm full of vampire power.

Cinitta sighs heavily when the power enters her, and her cheeks pinken.

"Thank you, queen," she says, looking up at me with beautiful eyes.

"You don't have to call me that," I tell her. "Not you." I touch her face, and she smiles.

"If you require anything, anything at all—" Francis is cut off as a girl runs into the house and comes to a stop in front of her.

"The vampires' homes are all on fire. Most of them are dead," she says while gasping for breath. I turn away when Francis looks at me.

"Queen." I don't answer, I just continue to observe. "Did you do this as a gift to us?"

A gift?

I guess witches would see it that way, considering vampires love our blood, and we hate them.

"She did," Cinitta says. "A display of her powers."

"Of course... of course." Francis nods as the young girl stares at me.

"I heard you are the daughter of the Devil."

Francis slaps her hard across the face. "You will not say such things out loud, child." The girl starts crying and runs off. Francis looks at me. "I'm sorry for my niece. She will not say such things again."

"Why? It's true," I reply with a smile.

Chapter Twenty-Two

TATIANA

We've been running for days. I'm tired, and half our people have died. John has lost hope. He's angry, hurt, and desperate. I get it, I really do. But we have never dealt with something this powerful before. And no matter what traps and tricks we leave for it, it always finds a way through to get to us.

"It will kill us all," one of the wolves says as we continue to walk. My feet are sore, almost to the point of bleeding. Our only hope now is to try our family home, hoping that maybe a witch old enough has dealt with something like this before or knows of something we haven't tried yet.

We first have to make our way through the vampire quadrant, which is not a smart thing to do with wolves, especially with our numbers dwindling. But we have no choice. It's the only way to get to the witches' quadrant. We could try our luck and ask a vampire if they know what we're dealing with, but I'm not sure they would give us answers, considering they hate our kind. Vampires only care about themselves and love power, probably equally as much as they love each other. The only thing they love more is blood, and we're walking blood bags going into their area.

It's not the smartest thing to do, but we have children with us, and going the long way around is incredibly hard to do with little ones who can't climb by themselves.

One of the wolves up front yells out to John. He checks on me before he runs off, then they stand at the top of the hill, scanning the area ahead. We all watch them, unsure of what is happening but not wanting to move, just in case. I watch as John turns around and waves, indicating for us to follow. When we get to the top of the hill, we all stop and look down.

What was once one of the most beautiful areas in Cardia is now nothing but burned piles of ash and rubble. Houses that were better than the ones we lived in growing up are still on fire. I've never seen this much destruction before, and I know who did it in my heart. We should be thankful, but I have a feeling that's only going to cause more trouble than it's worth.

"Your sister." John looks back at me.

"We can't be sure," I reply.

"You don't have to defend her any longer. We know it's her."

"She may be the only one to help us. Have you thought of that?" I ask. "She has been to the other world. I'm guessing that's where these things are from. She may know what to do with them or even how to kill them."

John simply stares at me, and I know he wants to say something else, but he bites his tongue and simply nods his head before he picks up one of our daughters and starts walking. I follow close behind, not saying a word.

I glance back at Tanya and see the dread filling her eyes. She also knows who did this. We both do. We just didn't actually think she would go through with it. Talia is not a cruel person. If anything, she is soft and forgiving and is always looking out for other people. I remember a time when it physically pained her to take someone else's life. And yet here I am, sure she has taken many. Granted, they were probably already dead, seeing as how they were vampires, but still, they were considered living beings on this plane.

"What else will she do?" Tanya asks me quietly as Melvon goes down to one house and stops in front of it. He comes back with a band and slides it on his wrist.

"It was my mother's. That was my house." He

nods to the rubble, and Tanya leans her head on his shoulder. "She died many, many years ago. But I always kept this." He holds up his wrist. "Your sister has caused a lot of death and destruction," he says.

Speaking of Death.

"Do you think *he* knows?" I ask Tanya.

"I don't know." She shrugs, knowing who I am speaking about.

Death is always there for her, but I wonder if that has altered now.

Max's death has changed her, and as I look around, I'm not sure it's for the best.

* * *

"Rest, my love. You need to rest." John takes the baby from my arms and nods for me to sit. We are close now to the witches, but as I look down, I see my swollen feet.

Melvon carries Tanya when she gets too sore, but I just keep walking. John has everyone to protect, so he doesn't need to worry about me as well.

"We're close," I tell him.

"We've seen no sign of that thing, so rest for a bit. I'll stand guard." He leans down and kisses my head. I remove my shoes and see a pool of blood in one, so I grab the bottle of water and start washing the cuts.

"She will be okay, though, right?" Tanya asks. I look over and see her biting her nails.

"What do you mean?"

"She will still be our sister. We still love her, no matter what she does."

I think about her words. Yes, we will always love her, but some things you can't come back from.

"Your opinion of her has changed. I want to say it's from when she saved your baby, but I have a feeling it happened when you found out who her father is."

"I still love her," I say. "That will never change. And one day, when you have kids, you will understand when I say she isn't my first priority anymore... my kids are." Tanya looks away. "What? What is it?"

"I won't have kids, Tatiana. Vampires don't reproduce."

"I'm sorry, I wasn't thinking."

"That's okay. It seems to be going around a lot lately."

"Witches." I turn to see Valefar, dressed impeccably as always, with a sinister smile attached to his lips. "It seems your sister is causing quite the stir in Hell." He waggles his brows. "Not that I'm not happy, but it's making me look bad, you know."

"Why are you here?" I ask him.

"Your sister has a throne now. Did you know?" I glance at Tanya, confused, before I look back to Valefar. "She is meant to be queen. It's her destiny. But a good queen is what she should've been, not what she is right now."

"And what is she right now?" I ask. His red eyes lock on mine.

"She is cruel," he says, the smile now gone. "You have seen the terror she caused here. Go and fix her. She's all wrong right now."

"And what if we can't? What if we have to kill her?"

"Tatiana," Tanya yells at me. "We will *never* kill her. Think of your baby."

"Okay, what if we have to imprison her?"

"You won't be able to do that again. She would never fall for it, and she is way too strong now to let that happen." John walks over and growls at Valefar, who isn't affected by him. "You need to get her to deal, and I'm afraid to say it, but I don't know if you can."

"So why come to us?" I ask him, and he looks over his shoulder.

"That york that has been following you is closer now, and I would prefer you to reach your sister before it kills you all." He claps his hands. "Up now. I would suggest you run."

I slide my shoes back on and do just that.

Chapter Twenty-Three

TALIA

"Someone is coming," Cinitta says as she steps out the front door.

I get up and follow her. "Who?"

"Your sisters," she replies, unsure. "With the wolves," she adds.

"We should welcome them." I smile as I head to the barrier to greet them. My sisters don't even bother smiling when they see me.

That's not very nice.

As they approach, Tatiana tentatively extends her hand out and touches the barrier. It shakes under her hand but doesn't move.

"Are you going to let us in?" she asks.

"Why are you here?" I ask. "This is the witches' quadrant."

238

"You opened a portal," one of the wolves yells, and I can hear the anger in her voice.

"I did no such thing." I smile.

Tatiana glares at me.

"You did, and you let something into our world."

"Like?" I ask with a lift of my brow.

"A york."

"Oh, really?" I look back to Cinitta. "Do you know what a york is, Cinitta?" She shakes her head. "It's something that can take the form of someone you loved and lost in order to suck your soul from your body and kill you."

"That doesn't sound good," Cinitta replies.

"It's killed half our people," Tatiana adds.

"Your people?" I tilt my head. "Are we not your people anymore?"

"You know you are."

"But you said... *your* people."

"The vampires killed all Max's people." My heart skips a beat at the sound of his name. I shake my head and step back. "I'm sorry you had to see that, Talia. That you had to go through that loss." Her hand pushes against the barrier, and I feel it in me as she does it. "Let us in." I study her for a moment and then drop the barrier. Everyone walks in, and I put it back up when the last of them is through. She steps close to me, and I smile at her, leaning in near her ear.

"It would be best if you didn't speak his name to me again."

She looks at me as if I am a stranger standing in front of her and not her sister, and she is partly correct. I'm not the pushover I once was—I'm a new woman, and I enjoy who I have become.

Max may have had a small part in it, and while my sister had a larger part, I still don't ever want to hear her say his name.

It hurts.

And I prefer not to deal with the pain.

I enjoy living here again, though it's not the same as it was. The house is different now. It has real food that we didn't have to go to a market to buy. The witches don't have to fear for their lives because I plan to protect them, as I have been doing. I always thought we would grow old here, but now I think that will only be me. I plan never to leave this place. It is where I see the rest of my life. And whether my sisters want to be a part of that will be completely up to them. I won't force them to stay, but I also won't force them to leave because, at one stage, this was home to all of us.

Tatiana looks around, confused, as the witches gather behind me. They're all in a stance that speaks volumes of who they are here to protect. Her eyes scan each of them before they land back on me. She wants to say something but bites her tongue, not voicing it.

She is probably the second-most powerful witch here —after me, that is—and most of these witches know it.

"Do you think of me as a threat, sister?" she asks.

I smile and lean in to touch her, and John growls. At his reaction, the witches raise a spell into the air.

Tatiana leans back and touches John's shoulder. "It's okay," she assures him before she looks back at me. "You would have them harm me? You would allow it?" she asks.

"No, of course not. I let you in, did I not?"

"You did, but I feel it comes with consequences." She pauses, a frown marring her features. "Have you spoken to Death?"

"Grim. And no, I have not."

"You loved him," she pushes, and I bite my cheek.

"I loved him, yes. And I loved someone else. So what is your point?"

"He may know how to help us."

Something hits the barrier.

We turn toward the sound, and I see him.

Standing there, looking at me. How easy it would be to walk up to the barrier and reach out and take his hand. A part of me wants to. To let it all down and watch as he walks to me and wraps his arms around my waist, and picks me up as his lips touch mine.

I miss Max.

And even though I know it's a york standing on the other side of that barrier, it doesn't mean that my heart rate doesn't pick up at the mere sight of him. He looks exactly as I remember. Even when he smiles at me, it's soft, and I know it's just for me. I want to reach out, but an arm wraps around my waist and pulls me back. When I turn, I see the real Grim standing tall amongst the frozen wolves and witches. He doesn't smile or even speak.

I raise my hands, and before I know it, they are smacking his chest, hitting him over and over again. He lets me, not bothering to move as I strike him.

I hate him.

I hate that he just left me there to deal with everything.

It's unfair and simply not right.

"Max told me to tell you something."

My hands pause at his words. "What?"

"I took Max, little fighter. You would have known that." He reaches out and wipes away a tear I didn't know had fallen.

"You saw him?" I ask on a choked breath.

"Yes." He nods, and then he drops to his knees in front of me, leaning forward until his head rests against my stomach. I'm so confused, but my hand lifts and lands in his hair, stroking through it. "I'm sorry for your loss. Your pain screams at me."

I pause the movement of my fingers sifting through his locks. "It does? Then why didn't you come sooner? It's been weeks since his death." The last word physically hurts as it leaves my mouth.

He remains where he is, head pressed against me. This is a new side of Grim I have never experienced, and I don't know how to feel about it all.

"I didn't expect to see this." I turn to the sound of that voice and see Lucifer with his black wings extended wide behind his back. His eyes lock on me. "You are in love with Death." Grim pulls away and stands. His hand finds mine and clamps around it, squeezing it tight. Lucifer's eyes fall on our joined hands. "Why are you here, old friend? You know this can never work."

"I stayed away."

"Have you, though?" Lucifer nods. "You know what will happen if you fall for a witch. You will be cast out. Do you really want to risk that?" he asks. "You take great pride in what you do, and you have been doing it long since before she was even a thought." I look over to Grim and see him already watching me.

"I stayed away," he repeats.

"So you said," Lucifer replies. "I can't approve of this." He shakes his head and looks at me. "You are not meant to rule with an Angel by your side. It's your birthright and no one else's. Ask him who is by your side when you die. Go on... ask him."

Grim looks away from my questioning gaze.

"Why so quiet, old friend?" Lucifer presses, stepping closer. When he reaches us, he halts. His eyes zoom in on my face before they track down to my stomach and then to Grim. "You knew?" Lucifer accuses.

I turn to Grim, confused.

"Do you plan to tell her? She has a right to know," he growls out the words. "Do you want me to drag you to Hell with me, friend, because I will. No god of yours will stop me once he knows."

I step away from Lucifer as his face hardens. This man is scary, and I would like to keep my body intact.

Grim shakes his head and glares at Lucifer. "You need to leave."

"Not until you tell her," Lucifer snaps at him. "Tell her, Grim." That is the first time I have heard any other person other than me use his name.

Grim looks at me, unsmiling. He grabs my hand again and lifts it. "I—" He stops himself, glances over his shoulder, and shakes his head.

Lucifer moves quickly, grabbing Grim and throwing him like he weighs absolutely nothing. Lucifer storms past me and reaches Grim as he stands again. This time, Grim stops his hit and moves out of the way.

"Tell her... or I will." Lucifer grabs his shoulder and pulls him back, throwing him into a tree. Hard. The tree cracks and somehow doesn't fall over.

"Stop it!" I scream, but they ignore me as they fly at each other.

Lucifer's wings flap harshly, and I watch in awe as Grim's black wings unfurl around him as they fight. I stand there, frozen, unsure what to do or how to stop them.

Do I even stop them?

Is that what I am meant to do? My hands clench at my side as I watch helplessly.

"Stop it, please," I try again, and this time, Grim looks over at me. Lucifer manages to get in a hit, knocking him backward and cracking his jaw.

"He has to tell you," Lucifer insists. "He has to."

"He will. Just stop hitting him," I beg.

Lucifer nods and steps back as Grim stands before me once again.

"Grim." My voice cracks on his name.

"What happened to you, little fighter? I've seen what you have done. You can't keep doing that," he whispers as he reaches me.

"I'll stop," I say.

He pushes my hair behind my ear.

I want to compare his touch to Max's.

But I can't.

They are both so different.

"What did he say to you?" I ask Grim.

He licks his lips before his silver eyes find mine. "He wants you to be happy. He said that's all he has ever wanted." Tears fill my eyes. "And that he is glad you found him. He said he would have died a thousand deaths if it meant he could have you once."

I can't stop the tears as they fall.

Grim lifts a hand and attempts to make them disappear from my face, but it's useless. Hearing Max's words, I can envision them leaving his lips as he whispered in my ear. That was the man I fell in love with. But as I look into Grim's eyes, I realize how lucky I am not to have loved one incredible man but two of them. I don't know what to say to him, and he seems as lost as I am as he wipes away my tears.

Lucifer stands behind us, quiet for once.

Grim's hands leave my cheeks, dropping low until they touch my stomach. He offers me a sad smile before he leans in and kisses my forehead softly. I'm confused by what is happening, but I don't bother stopping him. I welcome his touch.

Lucifer coughs, and I know he is pushing Grim to tell me what he thinks I should know. It feels like forever before Grim finally opens his mouth, and when he does, the words that escape rock me to my core.

I want to argue with him, tell him he doesn't know what he's talking about, but as I look past him to Lucifer, I know that his words are true. Even if I wish they weren't.

"You're pregnant."

He cups my face, trying to pull words from me, but I'm too speechless right now to come up with anything to say.

How does he know that I may be pregnant?

How does Lucifer know?

And why am I the last to know?

"Little fighter," he says, his eyes searching me for something, anything.

"Tell her the rest," Lucifer commands.

The rest? Is that not a big enough bombshell? I'm not sure I can handle any more life-altering news. I shake my head, then turn to the barrier where the york stands, pretending to be Max.

The thing is, the york isn't frozen like everyone else. It paces back and forth, watching us. I hate the fact that it can take on Max's face as if it has a right to his gorgeous form.

I focus back on Grim, waiting for him to continue. I'm not sure what else he could say.

"Grim." He sucks in a breath as I say his name. "Is the baby Max's?"

"No, it's mine," he chokes out.

The Angel of Death and a witch from Cardia have created a life. I'm sure there'll be stories told of this, poems possibly written, but the only thing I can think of is that it's not Max's. I'm not sure why it matters so much when I never even wanted children in the first place. Maybe it's because a part of me wants to keep him with me forever, even knowing that's not possible.

"She's disappointed," Lucifer says in observation, and it pulls me from my thoughts.

The thing with Max's face calls out my name, and I glare at it, mad at how it can possibly stand there and pretend to be something it's not. It's not fair, and all it does is make me angry. I face Grim, but before I can say anything, he is gone, and the world is moving again.

It doesn't take Tatiana long to figure out what happened when she sees I'm no longer in the last place she saw me. She picks up the baby and walks over to me, then lays her hand on my shoulder before she lifts it and wipes away the tears still falling from my eyes. I almost forgot they were there until that thing calls my name again.

When we turn toward it, we see it is now our mother staring back at us, offering us a soft smile and telling us to come and give her a cuddle. I can see how these things can destroy a world, but what do they do when it's only them left?

I look at my sister's baby and wonder if I'll be a good mother. I can't believe I even have that thought.

"What happened?" Tatiana asks.

I don't answer her.

I can't.

So I do the only thing I can do.

I turn and go back inside, locking myself in a room.

Chapter Twenty-Four

GRIM

"You love her." Lucifer stands behind me. "Yet, you left her," he adds. "Don't think I'm not aware that you left after getting free of Viper, just to what? Leave her there and die?" he yells from behind me.

I spin around to face him. "Since when do you care for anyone but yourself?" I ask angrily. I've known Lucifer for an incredibly long time before he became the King of Hell. We were once great friends—funny how times change.

"Things change, we change. As you are well aware," he says with narrowed eyes. "Why did you leave her?"

I turn away once more as we stand in the in-between. I come here often because of her. I tried to let her go because it was the right thing to do, even if it killed a part of me to see her happy with another.

Despite my hate for him, Maxilliam loved her with everything he was.

Gave her a love I was never able to.

"I was being called," I tell him truthfully. As soon as I was free from that room, I was pulled in every direction possible. I am Death, and souls were screaming for me everywhere. I couldn't stay there any longer. No matter what I wanted, I had no choice.

"See, that's where you are lying. You were called. Yes, we understand who you are, old friend. You forget I've been there. And I get you may have the hardest job of any of us, but sometimes you don't have to listen. You can make your own choice."

"No, you cannot."

"I'm proof you can."

"And look where that got you."

"He would never rid you of your role, and you know it. You have proved to be a loyal servant for years. You don't think he would know of her? We all know, old friend. So start putting her first." He is gone before I have a chance to say anything back.

The first time I saw Talia, she was nothing but a child. I didn't come to her because of any reason other than whispers of a great power. No one knew it was her, but I had already been searching for the person who it was foretold would rule this world and everyone in it.

I protected her without really understanding the reason why, visiting her as she got older, and she would tell me things about herself. And I remember thinking *she deserves to be queen, this one*. But first, she has to live.

And then, into her adulthood, I could see she started to look at me differently, and I didn't quite understand it at first. I had never dealt with anyone other than Angels, and they never experienced lust, love, or anything of the sort. It wasn't until she kissed me that I experienced it in full force. It was a mistake. I knew the moment it happened, and yet I did absolutely nothing to stop it. I had warned her that we could not work, and when she got lost in that portal, I went mad looking for her. Until one day, she reappeared. But she was not alone.

She had grown in her time away, and it was obvious by the single look that she gave me, and the man standing behind her, that things were different. I realized those green eyes that held so many secrets of mine didn't look at me the same.

It's unusual and extremely rare for an Angel to fall in love, but that's what I have done.

And now she is pregnant.

It would be easier if the baby wasn't mine. But I

knew the moment I heard the heartbeat whose baby it was. It's one of the joys of being who I am. I know everyone's death and when they will die. I even know my own son's death.

And I know when that day comes, his mother won't be far behind.

Chapter Twenty-Five

TALIA

My sisters come into my room separately, both trying to work out what happened the other day. But I still can't wrap my own mind around it, so I'm not sure how I'm supposed to explain it to them.

I lie in a bed that's foreign to me but that I welcome all the same. It's a big difference from the bed I had growing up in this house. This mattress has springs, it's not on the floor, and it even has a headboard and sheets, plus a blanket and pillows.

My mind has been reeling. How was this even possible? That I didn't know.

Correction, I *should have* known that this could happen.

When Grim whispered the words that I was pregnant, I didn't automatically think the baby was his. Instead, my mind drifted straight to Max, and for a moment, just a slight moment, I wanted to smile, thinking that I still had a piece of him with me. But the world doesn't work that way. It gives you what you deserve and what you can handle.

I caress my belly. How could I not have known? It's been months, and I didn't even stop to think that I could be pregnant. The time in this world is different from the time I spent with Max in his world, and I try to work it all out in my head. But I come up with nothing.

Cinitta checks on me often.

None of them knows what is happening. They don't quite understand how I went from the person who was constantly moving and doing things to someone who just lies silently in bed. I think they know Grim has something to do with it, though.

"Talia." Tatiana sits at the edge of my bed and offers me a smile as she lays her hand on my foot. "You have to talk. What happened?"

"Is John still afraid for you to be around me?" I ask.

She's taken aback by my comment, but shakes her head. "No. He just didn't know what to expect."

I sit up, my back against the headboard. She goes to speak, but the air in the room changes, and she freezes.

Grim appears, a weird look on his face that I'm not sure I'm ready to deal with. But a weird sense of relief floods over me at the sight of him.

"I loved him. Did you know that?" I ask Grim, and he nods. "I loved you as well," I whisper.

"I know." He steps closer, lifts the sheets, and climbs into bed next to me. He pulls me to him with ease, as if we were made to fit perfectly with each other. "But we have eternity together. You will outlive everyone you love," he whispers.

I hate that thought—it sends a shiver through my body.

And I hate that I love them both.

Everything has happened so fast, and it's all-consuming.

"You haven't been sleeping," he says, his hand stroking my hair. I lay my head on his chest, and I'm met with a smell that brings me more comfort than I care to admit. "I need you to sleep." He kisses the top of my head. "I'll stay here with you."

I flick my gaze to my sister's frozen form and close my eyes. And when I do, I dream of a world where everyone I love is alive, well, and happy.

As I wake with a jump, Grim holds me tighter.

"You are safe," he says, kissing the top of my head.

"I killed all those vampires."

"You did," he whispers.

"Does that make me an evil person?" I ask. He remains silent. "Grim?"

"No, it just means you are more human than you thought. And sometimes humans snap under pressure." I take his excuse and hold it close to my chest. It's all I can think of doing.

"I have to tell them, don't I?" I lift my head to gaze at him, and his eyes shift to my sister before they look back at me.

"That is up to you."

"If I asked you to take me from this world, would you?"

"No."

"Why?" I look up at him through my lashes.

"Because this world needs you more so than I do." He kisses the top of my head, and then he is gone.

"Talia." I turn to my sister. "What's wrong?" she asks, and I shake my head.

"Everything," I whisper. She moves up the bed and sits next to me. I don't tell her that Grim was just here.

"I heard about Max." Her expression is sorrowful.

"I'm sorry. I know you two had something serious."

"Yeah."

"I'm sorry about John as well. He just thought—"

"That I was crazy."

"Well, you were a little."

"Fair call," I say, nodding.

"That york is still out there. It keeps on forming into our mother." I quiver at the thought. "Francis really admires you. I never thought that old bat would admire anyone."

"Francis has been good to me. She helped restore this house," I say, looking around.

"I wouldn't say restore... it's practically brand new. Nothing like what we grew up in." She laughs.

The door opens, and Tanya spots us in bed before she walks in and shuts the door behind her. She climbs on the bed with us.

"You are both smiling. I like it." I look to Tatiana and smile wider. "It's good to see you both smile again. It's been too long." I turn to Tanya and ask, "Does Melvon hate me for killing his people?"

"They killed all of Max's people, so no."

"Oh my God." I shake my head.

"So you probably did a good thing."

"It doesn't feel good. And his people... they just wanted a better life, and look what happened," I whisper, sinking into the bed. "I feel like all I bring is destruction and death."

"You don't, not at all. You bring so much more. And you know it." Tatiana holds my hand. "Look at my daughter. She was dead, and you gave her life. Now she is breathing and in her father's arms, fast asleep."

"You hated me for what I did," I whisper.

"Yes, that was hard. Because even though you did the right thing, it hurts to know she won't get a full life."

I bite my lip at her words.

"What?" she asks.

"Grim said something to me."

"What did he say?"

It's sad, but I know a part of her will get relief from it.

"That I will outlive you all." I watch as the words I have said register in her mind. She can't believe it at first. Then her eyes gloss over, and she leans down and kisses my cheek.

"I'm happy and sad to hear that. Sad that you will have to watch us all die, but happy that my daughter will get a full life."

"A long life," I whisper to her.

"Yes, a long and happy life."

"I have to ask you both something. I don't want you to freak out, but I've been thinking about this for a while now," Tanya says, crossing her legs as she sits at the end of the bed. She looks down at her nails and starts to play with them. Just as she goes to speak, the door opens, and John peeks his head in. He looks around until his eyes fall on his mate, then he nods and steps back out.

"Checking up on you." I smile at Tatiana.

"He always does that, no matter who I'm with," she says. "It's one of the many reasons I love him."

"Speaking of love." We both turn back to Tanya, who is still playing nervously with her nails. "I want to ask your opinion on something. Actually, I think my mind is set, but I still trust what you both have to say."

"Um... okay," I reply, confused.

"What is it, Tanya?"

"I want to become a vampire."

Holy mother of God.

Did she just say that? No, she couldn't have.

Why?

"Both of your faces are scaring me. Why are you looking at me like that? My partner is one, and he will outlive me. I will continue to age while he stays the same. I don't want that. I want forever with him," she whines.

"What does Melvon say about this?" I ask her.

Tatiana turns to me, shock written on her face. She

does not approve in the slightest of this idea. But I have a feeling it's no longer an idea and just a matter of time before it becomes a reality.

"Who cares what Melvon says? This can't happen. You can't become a vampire. If you do, you will lose your natural abilities."

"Let's be honest... my powers are nothing compared to either of yours. I've always been the lesser sister. The one they kidnap, the one no one sees as a threat. Melvon sees me as so much more than any of that. He is the first person to ever do so, and I want to spend eternity with him."

"You aren't a nobody. We see you," I insist.

"Yes, you see me," she agrees fondly. "But no one else ever has. No one has said, 'Hey, those sisters are a real hoot, especially that middle one.'" Tanya rolls her eyes.

"I think it's stupid. Why would you want to be reliant on someone else's blood? Do you want Melvon to drink from someone else? I know you enjoy him drinking from you," Tatiana says, crossing her arms over her chest.

"I do."

"So you want to watch as he drinks from someone else?" Tatiana bites back at her.

Tanya tears at her nails as she lowers her head. "I didn't think of it like that."

"No, you didn't. But I did. You will have a great life together. Why must you think about ending it in that manner."

"You just hate vampires," Tanya gripes.

"I like Melvon," Tatiana replies.

"No, you don't. If you could pick anyone else for me, you would."

"You're right, I would. But that isn't my choice. It's yours. But this is crazy, even for you."

"For me?" Tanya sits up straighter at Tatiana's words. "What's that meant to mean?" Tanya asks her.

"It means you are stupid for even thinking about it."

"I am not. You are stupid for letting our sister save your baby and then being mad at her for it!" she screams. I sink farther into the bed. "Worry about your own life and not mine." Tanya stands to leave, but I call her name. She pauses with her hand on the doorknob.

"Maybe just wait for a while," I suggest. "There's no harm in waiting. What does Melvon say about it?"

"He doesn't want me to do it," she says into the door. "But I want it. Doesn't that count for anything?"

"Yes, of course, but I think he may be right. For now, at least," I say gently.

"I wanted both of your support on this," she whispers, her back still to us. "It's sad that I don't get it."

"You wanted us to blindly accept the fact that you want to be a vampire?" Tatiana says. "No, we will not do that. We love you and don't want that for you." Tanya doesn't say another word as she opens the door and walks out.

Tatiana glares at me. "I don't know what's going on with you, but you need to get out of this bed as well." She gets up and stalks to the door. "And I expect you to tell me what you are hiding. I know it's something." She closes the door as she walks out.

And with that, I sink into the bed as a blood-curdling scream rips through the house.

Chapter Twenty-Six

I leap from the bed and run out of the house to see the york has someone on the other side of the barrier. *How did they get them?*

John is standing there, his fists closed at his sides, as he watches it all play out in front of us. The york grabs the person by the throat—it seems to smile in whatever form it's taken—and leans in. It appears to be kissing the person, but it's not. It is sucking the life right out of them.

John turns to face me when I reach him, my sisters already by his side.

"Do you know how to stop it?" he asks.

"I don't."

Neither did Max. But I guess someone has to try. It can't remain here.

"You don't look so sure. We can't let it stay here

and consume people one by one. We have to try something."

"Max found a way to keep them out of the village in the other world," I say. "I'm guessing it was a barrier like this." I point to the one that's currently up.

"It still managed to get one of yours." When I look back, the york drops the witch to the ground in an unmoving heap. No soul in their body left, which means... no person left.

"I can ask Lucifer," I offer, and everyone goes silent.

"That may be a good idea. He's old enough where he might understand what this is."

"Maybe you should try Valefar instead," Tatiana suggests.

"You think he's more trustworthy than Lucifer?"

"Lucifer is the King of Hell, and he never bothered to see you until recently. And he's what? Simply willing to help you now. Seems a little odd." She shrugs her shoulders. "That's all I'm saying."

"I don't trust either of them, but Lucifer is more forthcoming than Valefar," I tell her.

I think of Lucifer. But before I go, I offer a smile, and then I'm transported to a place I haven't seen before.

"Oh my God." I cover my eyes and scream as I turn away. On the bed in the middle of the room is Lucifer

T.L SMITH

and a thing. Is that a woman? It has scales—red bumpy scales—all over, and Lucifer is fucking it. Oh my God, I can't believe I just saw that.

"This is an unexpected visit today," Lucifer croons. "Drogan, you can leave. It seems my daughter needs me so desperately that she forgot to knock." I spin around to see him with pants on now. Thank God.

"I didn't know. I just... I thought of you and ended up here," I explain.

Drogan gets up from the bed, not a care in the world that she is naked. Her breasts are hard and scaly, and she has no hair on her body. She gives me a sour look, and I place my hands on my hips.

"Drogan, you wouldn't be giving my daughter attitude, would you?" Lucifer asks and turns back to face her. She smiles at him and rolls her eyes before she leaves the room without a backward glance.

"I didn't know," I say again.

"I can tell. Now, what is so urgent for you to be here?" He goes over to a dresser, and I take in the room. It's all black with a red bed and a red drawer set. Plain and boring but a statement, nonetheless.

"Is this your room?" I ask.

"No, it's my fuck room."

Well, okay. I shouldn't have asked if I didn't want the answer.

"Yorks. Have you heard of them?"

"You mean that thing you almost touched before Grim got to you?"

"Yes, that."

"How is it going with Grim, by the way? Have you spoken to him?"

"No. And I don't wish to discuss that right now. I came for help, not questions."

He nods and sits at the end of the bed. "Yorks are a myth. They have never existed in this world, but I do know stories of them," he says with a grin.

"Can you please share?"

"For you? Of course."

"Why are you so nice to me?" I blurt out. The stories about him and who he is don't add up.

"Would you prefer me not to be?" he questions, looking amused.

"Well, no?" I say, unsure. "I just wasn't sure if it's a trick or..."

"No, it's anything but. I liked your mother. And I see a lot of her in you. And if you care to know a secret... you are quite powerful, and it makes me proud," he boasts.

"Thank you," I say, the compliment warming me.

"You're welcome. Now, to the stories of yorks. They are an entity, meaning they aren't quite real, but they can take the form of those who have passed on. The stories say the way to kill them is to wait until they take a form, and then someone who has the ability to absorb the same way they do, or in the form of the way they do, has to absorb them. Where they take the life-force, you need someone to take theirs."

"I can do that."

"No, you cannot risk that. Have you forgotten something?" He motions to my stomach. "The heart-beat is loud. And while I get the feeling you haven't told anyone yet, people will be hearing it soon, and you are starting to show." I look down at my stomach and notice a small bump. "Your wolves will hear it soon enough."

"Possibly," I tell him. "Thank you. I won't drop in like this again."

He waves me off. "You are always welcome wherever I am, but next time, try to aim for the other side of the door." He winks, and I smile before I leave.

When I get back, everyone is standing where I left them, waiting for me. It's utterly still and silent.

"He only knew of myths," I tell John.

Tatiana walks over and grips his arm.

"Myths?" he questions, confused.

"They aren't from this world," I remind him.

"Okay. So what did he know?"

"That the way to kill one is the same way they kill... by taking what is theirs." I turn toward it, and as it locks eyes with me, it morphs into Max. He smiles, and

I want to run over and hold his hand and let him wrap his arms around me so tightly I can't breathe. Everything in me wants that, but I remain where I am, knowing full well that thing is not Max.

"You can't do it. It could kill you. We aren't even sure that's the right way to kill it," Tatiana says. "You could die. We can't go out to help you either. We can't risk it. We need to find another way."

"And let it keep luring people out?" I push.

She shrugs. "If they are silly enough to believe it, knowing what it does, we can't stop that."

"I don't want people to die," I whisper.

"You killed enough yourself," one of the wolves says.

I wince at the hate in its voice.

"That's enough," John roars. The witches look at him before they focus on me. "You will respect Talia," he says. "She is queen." Everyone goes quiet. The witches nod their heads in agreement, but the wolves grumble in discontentment.

"She is not *our* queen."

"But she is," he argues. "She is queen to us all, and you will respect her, or you will be at her mercy. We wanted a ruler who would be fair, and this is what we got."

"You are our ruler," one of the wolves says.

"I am your alpha, and I will always be, but this is

T.L SMITH

our queen." Someone starts clapping, and we all turn to see who it is. When the crowd parts, we see Valefar grinning at us.

"What a great speech. And it's expected for every queen to go a little crazy like your new one did. I mean, she did almost destroy an entire race." He smiles and looks at Melvon. "Tell me, do you hate your new queen?" Everyone waits to hear what Melvon will say.

He turns from Valefar and faces me. "She is our queen," he says.

"That wasn't the question I asked. But that is enough of an answer for me to know you do," Valefar states.

Tanya turns her confused expression on Melvon, then reaches for him. He leans down and whispers in her ear, and she shakes her head at his words and looks back at me.

Valefar turns to study the york. When he does, it transforms from Max into an unfamiliar man. Valefar approaches the barrier, careful not to come into contact with it. The york says his name and reaches for him.

"I heard Father speaking of this," he says and nods to it. "I wanted to see him one last time." I come up and stop beside him. "He was a demon, an amazing one. Climbing up the ladder, as you might say." He laughs. "I would dare say he could have given me a run for my money, but we all know that's a lie. I'm amazing." He winks at me and looks back at the york. "I loved him. As much as a demon can love someone with a black heart."

"How did he die?" I ask.

"Witches," he replies, his eyes still on the york. "They trapped him and killed him."

"I'm sorry."

"What Father forgot to tell you, or perhaps didn't know, is that in order to take from it as it does from you, you need to make it whole." I wait for him to continue. "You think it's whole when it takes the form of someone, but it's not fully whole. You need to make it that way."

"And how do you do that?"

Valefar leans in close to my ear and whispers so only I can hear, "I can hear the heartbeat."

I suck in a breath at his words. He pulls away and smiles at me. "You need to make it whole by letting it touch you, but you also risk it taking from you." He looks at my stomach. "I'm guessing this is why Father warned you away." I nod my head. "You risk it taking another life before your own," he says on another low whisper.

I gasp and take a half step back.

The thing smiles at him, and Valefar turns to face me.

"Why are you helping me?" I ask.

"You will be the queen of this world, and one day I will be King of Hell. I think we'll be amazing allies." He winks before he disappears.

"What did he say?" Tatiana asks as she approaches.

"He told me how to kill it."

"And?"

"And... I think I can do it."

The york has once again turned into our mother, offering her hand to both of us. When we don't take the bait, I watch as it morphs into Patrick. Tatiana sucks in a breath next to me, not expecting that, and my heart hurts a little at seeing him.

"I have to do it. I don't know how they multiply, but we can't risk that happening. The other world had hundreds of them, Tatiana. We don't want that here." I turn to her. "Trust me... we don't want them here."

"Will it be safe?"

"Probably not, but under no circumstance can you help." She nods her head.

"You can do it. If anyone can, it's you." She gently squeezes my arm in a show of support, and I want to believe her.

I hope her words are true, but I'm confident about what I'm about to do. She doesn't know about the baby. If she did, would she still let me try?

I already know the answer to that.

Keeping it a secret is the only thing I can think of doing right now. So that's what I'll do until I know it's a good time to tell her.

When will that be? I have no idea.

But right now is not it.

Chapter Twenty-Seven

"How do you plan to do it?" John asks as he strides up to us.

"Walk over and hope I get to it first," I say, shrugging my shoulders. My plan is not great, but I have nothing else right now.

"Sounds like a great plan of attack," he says sarcastically.

"Uh-huh."

A small silver bird flies toward the barrier, and we watch as it goes straight through. And then comes directly to me, flying over my head.

"Is that..." John trails off in astonishment.

"Those amazing birds were in Max's world too," I whisper, my eyes widening in awe.

"It's a peachie. Correct?" he asks.

"Yes," I answer, remembering when Max told me about them. "They are attracted to power. They only go to those who hold the most." I repeat what Max once said.

He watches it flying over my head as I stare at the york.

"I have to do it," I whisper.

"We can always try to think of another way," John says.

"It's the only way. I'm sorry in advance if it doesn't work. I know you will be good to my sister, so that's all I ask."

"You'll do just fine. You always have." We look back to the york in the form of Patrick. "He knew it too. It's why he was willing to give his life for you, so let's honor him."

I suck in a breath before I face John. "Please get everyone back. If I can walk through the barrier, it may be able to come through too. I'm not quite sure how that works."

John steps away and tells everyone to get back. They all take several steps back, leaving me standing by myself at the barrier.

The fake Patrick smiles at me from the other side, and my hand lowers until it's resting on my stomach.

How can I not do this? I have to. Everyone is relying on me to get this done.

And as it seems I am the only one who may be able to right this wrong.

It's my fault the yorks are here. I opened the portal by mistake, and this is what came through. I watch the peachie flying over my head, and I give it a smile. It reminds me so much of Max that it makes my heart beat faster.

The spell I cast settles over me, licking my skin as my hand slides through the barrier. The york watches on in interest with Patrick's eyes. I manage to push my whole body through, and when I'm on the other side, I check back to ensure the area I went through closes directly behind me.

Taking my attention off the york is my first mistake. Because as I do, it reaches out and grabs my shoulder. My head swings around, and instantly I feel dizzy. I feel my power draining as it takes from me. So as quickly as I can, I shoot my hand out and grip its shoulder. It's then I hear a voice coming from behind me.

"You shouldn't have done that." Grim is so close that he's basically in my ear. A shiver racks through me at his nearness. "You shouldn't have let it touch you." His disgruntled groan makes it clear that I have made a big mistake.

I mirror what the york is doing, my hands taking its power while it is taking from me.

"Keep going," Grim commands.

I do, but I'm getting tired, and I feel the york draining me. Something settles on my stomach, and I know it's Grim's hand. "Keep going," he whispers into my ear.

I close my eyes and do as he says, concentrating all my efforts on this one task.

My legs shake, and the york pulls back but only slightly.

It's exhausting to keep this up, so much so that I am fighting now to keep my eyes open. I used to get tired when I would take power and give it back. But never when I only took—I found that caused me to be on a high. However, this power is not what I'm used to. It's laced with something different.

It tastes...

... damn awful.

I want to let go.

Every part of me is telling me to just let go.

But I know if I do, it will take from me as I am taking from it right now.

"Little fighter, hold on." I continue to do as Grim says.

The york changes into Max, startling me for a second, but I don't remove my hand, and I won't stop. I am concerned about how much of me it can take before there isn't much of me left.

Ice-blue eyes stare back at me.

I want to lean into them.

It smiles with Max's mouth, and that makes me angry.

How can it do that?

How can it play with me like that?

The loss of Max only makes me more determined.

I lift my other hand and grip its other shoulder. Its eyes go wide in surprise as I push even harder. It momentarily stops taking from me and tries to change shape. I watch as it flickers in front of my eyes, but now I have a strong hold on the york. I'm in charge, and it has just realized that.

Taking as much as I can, as quickly as possible, I watch as the york falls to its knees. I go down with it, still holding as I continue to take and take and take. It transforms back into a black mist, but the mist has substance now.

"You are doing so well," Grim says. "Finish him."

What other choice do I have? I need to do this if I want to live.

Max flashes into my mind, and I smile as I push harder.

He would want me to live, even if it meant without him by my side. So I suck, and I take as much as I can possibly take before everything goes black.

* * *

"Why isn't she waking? She should be awake by now. It's been days." I open my eyes to see Tatiana at the end of my bed, pacing back and forth as she talks to Tanya.

"We must be patient."

"The barrier is still up, so that's good, right?" Tatiana asks. "It means she still has power."

"I still have power... I think." I croak out the words, and both sets of eyes—the same color as mine—lock onto me.

"You're awake! Oh God, we were so worried." Tatiana rushes over and sits next to me. Her hand goes to my head to feel it before she pulls away and smacks me across the face.

I cringe, rearing my head back. "What the heck?" I hold my cheek, and she glares at me with her mouth set in a snarl. "Why did you do that?" She pulls the blankets away from my stomach and looks at me.

"Do you care to tell us about this?" Tanya leans over to see what Tatiana is questioning. I glance at my round stomach and protectively lay my hands on it.

"Are you pregnant?" Tanya asks, confused.

"It would seem so," I reply.

Tanya shakes her head as Tatiana swears.

"You did that..." She waves her hands around. "You risked your life and your unborn baby for what?"

"For all of you. Did I do it? Is that thing gone?"

"It is, but your barrier is still up, and those birds are still here, flying above the house."

"Who's the father?" Tanya asks.

"Grim, obviously," Tatiana says, and I raise an eyebrow in surprise.

"How did you know?"

"We could see you on the other side of the barrier, even when Grim was there. He was touching your belly, and you did as well. I knew then you were hiding something."

"I wasn't hiding it..." I take a deep breath. "I just didn't know how to tell you."

"How could you not tell us?" She looks down at my stomach, shaking her head in disbelief.

"I just didn't think." I shrug.

"You should have told us. It's a joyous occasion," Tanya adds.

I offer her a small smile, and she returns it, but hers is much bigger.

"I didn't intend to hide the fact I am pregnant. I just needed some time to absorb it. It was a lot to take in."

When I sit up, my head spins. I lift my hand to my

head and see markings decorating my arms. There are black swirls stuck to my skin like a tattoo.

"Yeah, we can't work out what that is. Does it hurt?" Tatiana asks as I study them.

They wrap around my arm and go all the way up to my shoulder. I pull my shirt off to see if they're anywhere else, but it doesn't appear as if they are.

"It doesn't hurt," I tell them, running a finger along one of the swirls. Then I look back at them. "It worked? Has it definitely gone?"

"You killed it. To be honest, it was the most amazing thing I have ever witnessed," Tanya whispers. "Just before you fell, that thing exploded, and the sky lit up. Black smoke rose, and a loud clap was heard before sparks rained down everywhere." Tatiana nods as Tanya describes what happened. "Grim picked you up and walked straight through your barrier, carried you to the house, and placed you in bed. He didn't leave until this morning. He's been here for days, and he was drained. He looked terrible, as if he needed..."

"Death," Tatiana finishes for her. "It's like he needs souls to survive in this world. He was almost vanishing in front of our eyes, if that's even the right word." She shrugs. "Anyway, he made sure we would stay by your side until his return. So here we are."

"Yeah, he's bossy," Tanya whispers, then giggles.

I smile at her words. *Grim, bossy?* He's always so misunderstood.

"So, it is his baby, right?" Tanya asks.

"I think so," I reply quietly.

"I mean... he would know," Tatiana says.

"He would." I nod and climb out of bed to stand on shaky legs. A loud thud is heard, and we look up at the roof.

"Those birds have been trying to get in ever since we brought you inside." Tatiana shakes her head. "They seem to be immune to spells as well."

"What did you do?" I ask.

"I tried a catching spell, which obviously didn't work because those things are still annoying."

"I want to go out and see them." Tanya helps me to the door and then leads me outside. John is out the front, talking to Francis when we reach the yard.

The birds start chirping louder, and we look at them as they fly in circles above my head.

"Hopefully, now those things will be quiet."

"Your belly." Francis gasps and points at my stomach.

Shit, I forgot to put my shirt back on, and all I am wearing is a crop top. I try to cover my belly with my hands, but it does no good. John pulls off his shirt and hands it to me. I smile gratefully as I accept and slide it on. "You are with child. It's a miracle," Francis says, head tilted to the sky and smiling.

The birds chirp louder and louder. I reach a hand up, and they start to circle around it, faster and faster, until I can't keep sight of them. I feel something happening, though, something changing or shifting. And when I open my eyes, I watch as the black swirls that were on my arm slide up to my fingertips and off my skin. A bird opens its mouth and sucks the swirls in as if they're food before they all fly off, straight through the barrier and out of sight.

"Did that just happen?" Tanya asks. "I mean, my eyes do play tricks on me and all."

"Oh, that happened," Tatiana adds. "Maybe that's why they were so crazy. They wanted to help." I smile at the thought. "How do you feel?" she asks me.

"Good. I mean... I still feel like me, which is good, right?"

"Yes, absolutely." She grabs my hand and leads me back toward the house. "I'll get you some food, and we can discuss names for the baby."

I stop at the entrance to find Grim pacing back and forth in front of my door. He pauses mid-step when he catches sight of me, his gaze exploring me from head to toe. "You're awake."

"I am."

He walks straight over and wraps his arms around

me, embracing me tightly, before he takes us away. I feel the world shift, and when I open my eyes, we are standing on our beach, our little piece of paradise.

"You are wearing another man's shirt," he grumbles and pulls back.

I look down at John's shirt before I glance at him. "Does it bother you?"

"It does. I was a good man... I let you go, but I can't do it twice." He steps up to me and touches my belly. "Not now. Not again."

"I'm not sure where we are, Grim. And you can't expect anything from me. I loved Max. You know that, right? That love doesn't simply go away." As my love for him, but I don't let that slip. He knows that, Grim will, and always will be a love for me. It pains and delights me all in one.

Grim nods his head in understanding. "I know. Just know I will happily wait a million lifetimes for you." He leans down and kisses my cheek before he takes me back. When we reappear, my sisters are waiting for me with food.

He doesn't stay, but that night he returns and every other night following. We hardly speak—he is just there, supporting me. Checking on me. During the day, he leaves to do what must be done.

I am unsure if he stays all night, every night, but

one night I woke in pain and saw him sitting there, reading my mother's diary.

I haven't kissed him.

Barely touched him.

But he never pushes.

Never asks.

He is just...

... there.

Chapter Twenty-Eight

As I stare into Brody's eyes, I can't believe he is mine.

I do this regularly—simply staring at our son.

He has my eyes, not Grim's, but it's clear as day who his father is. Brody looks almost identical to him, down to his nose and dark hair. He cries, and I lift him to me, cuddling him close.

So much has changed, and yet everything remains the same.

I am queen.

I have accepted the fact and have reveled in it, as it was my chosen path.

We no longer have a barrier up. People live where they choose, and life is... dare I say it, good.

Everything is good.

And it makes me incredibly happy.

Witches live where they choose. Some have stayed, while others have made their homes elsewhere. Tanya and Melvon live here, but Tatiana and John have gone back to where the wolves called home for so long. That's their habitat, and that's why they choose to call it home.

New paths have been made—with the help of magic—and we see each other regularly.

Grim is still the Angel of Death—that will never change. And to be honest, I'm not sure it should. He was created for that job, and it's all he knows. And when he is away from it for too long, I see that his body changes, and he loses a part of himself. I think it's the same way I am when I'm drained of my magic. I don't feel complete.

"Is he asleep?" Grim asks, appearing next to us.

I still live in the same house. It's funny how I am the only one left now. It's not the same as it was when we were growing up, though, so that makes me happy. It's mine, and now it is also our son's.

Francis has become someone I rely on heavily. Cinitta drops in when she can, but she now lives in the woods where we first met. She is as loyal as ever—it's one thing I admire about her.

"No, he is fussing," I tell Grim as I pace back and forth, trying to rock our son to sleep. Brody seems to only want to fall asleep when he's in someone's arms—preferably mine, but he loves being in Grim's as well. Grim takes him without even thinking and starts rocking gently, and it isn't long until he falls asleep.

We haven't spoken about us.

What we could be.

Or even what we are.

When Grim's here, we talk of our son, and that's it. He doesn't ask me how my day was, and to be honest, I like it this way. I needed time, and time is what Grim has given me.

I look at him, dressed in all black, and sit down as I watch them together. When I gave birth, Grim was right by my side. Francis delivered Brody, and straight after, my father appeared. He took one look, smiled, kissed the top of my head, and disappeared.

Grim made sure I was okay through the delivery, and before he even went to check on his son, he first ensured I was fine.

"He likes you more," he whispers to me, careful not to wake the baby.

When I don't say anything, Grim stops rocking and looks at me. "It's because you smell like his food." I nod my head in agreement. "I like you more too."

Grim's words shock me so much that I just sit there and stare at him. He smirks, and it makes my heart jump at the sight. He walks Brody to his crib, laying him down carefully. The sweet little Angel doesn't make a sound.

Grim straightens and walks over to me, offering me his hand. I look at it, wondering what he wants. "Come somewhere with me." I glance past him to our son. "He'll be fine. I can see him from anywhere in the world." I nod and manage to stand. When I place my hand in his, he transports us, and my bare feet land in the sand. I smile up at him as I sit down on the beach, the water lapping gently in front of me.

"I feel like I haven't left the house for ages," I say, relishing the feeling of being back here.

"I know."

"You do?"

Grim nods and sits beside me. "I want to kiss you," he says, and I turn to see his eyes on my lips. "But I won't ever kiss you without your permission," he whispers. His statements make my stomach flutter.

I've longed for those lips for so long, dreamed of them.

"What if I said you shouldn't ask?" I suck in a deep breath and continue. "You don't have to ask to kiss me, Grim. You should kiss me when you feel the need."

"You have been hurting," he says. "I didn't want to interfere with your healing."

"I'll always hurt. It's a part of this thing called life."

"Yes, I guess it is." And in the next moment, his

hands are in my hair as he presses closer. When his lips touch mine, it's soft at first, before they become more demanding. With a hum from my chest, he picks me up and places me on his lap. Our lips are sealed together, and as I open my mouth, not breaking the kiss, he slides his tongue in, tasting me. His hands travel from my head down my body until they reach my hips, and I savor the sensations he's reawakening within me.

I take his strong hands in mine, placing them on my breasts, which he happily allows, and he squeezes before he slips them under my shirt. As Grim massages my breasts, I grind my hips on him, back and forth, my lips moving with his in a way that has my body alight for more.

I wish I could do this forever.

I missed him.

I missed us.

I missed this.

A part of me always knew Grim was where my heart was, but the other part tried to fight it.

I always thought we could never work.

And maybe we still can't.

But we both seem to be trying.

I don't ask him to stop what he does, not that I even think he could. I would never ask him to.

This man is Death, after all.

And I am a witch who is in love with Death.

It's silly, really.

No matter the trials and tribulations we went through.

We were always meant to be.

I pull back and break our kiss, though reluctant. My body is on high alert and full of need.

For him.

I stand, pulling at my clothes. And when I'm naked, I sit back on his lap, my lips finding his once more. His searching hands grip my hips, pulling me flush against him before skimming all over my body.

I now have stretch marks on my stomach, and my boobs aren't the same anymore, but none of that matters to Grim. He touches and loves me without a care in the world.

The way he looks at me is the way every man should look at a woman.

With admiration.

Pride.

Lust.

I reach between us, but he beats me to it, and his hard cock pops out of his trousers. So I lift up on my knees and hover above him.

"Little fighter," he whispers into my ear before biting it. "If my death was to come tomorrow, I would die a happy man."

I throw my head back and laugh.

"But you are Death," I say. "So make me a happy woman."

"As you wish." He pulls me down, and I slide straight onto him. He's like home, and it feels like forever since we have had each other this way.

I almost feel guilty for feeling this with Grim because of Max.

Like it's betrayal.

My love for Max and Grim was different. I had hopes and dreams with Max, but with Grim, I just see us. I've always just seen us. It was he who had the issue.

He bites my shoulder as my hips rock against him. I throw my head back with moan after moan as each movement rocks me to my core. It feels good in every way possible.

"I'm never leaving you," he promises. "Not in this lifetime or the next."

My hips start moving faster and faster until everything inside of me combusts. I collapse onto his chest, and he holds me there.

"Brody," he says, and before I can say anything, we are back in my house, his cock still inside of me as he lays me on the bed. He slides himself back into his trousers and looks me over as I lay there naked. He seems to take mental images as he walks to the door, then turns back. "Stay there. We aren't finished." Then he goes for our son.

If you had asked me a year ago if this was how I saw my life, the answer would be a firm no.

I am queen, yes, but I also have a council of people to oversee the realm. They help with decision-making and running the realm. I am a new mother, after all, and I don't want to become power-hungry as Veronica did. On the other hand, I am incredibly astute about what power does to people, and I will ensure I never go down that destructive path.

There are no more tokens.

We work, and we get paid.

It's as simple as that.

No hunting or killing of any kind is allowed.

When I set that rule, Valefar showed up, unimpressed. Unfortunately, he likes to play games with the living, so I told him to leave. I have only seen him once when I caught him spying on Brody. He left him a teddy bear, and he was smiling down at him. I know I shouldn't trust either Valefar or Lucifer. But for some reason, I do.

Tanya has decided that being a vampire is not a priority. Yet. And she has found a love for healing, in which she is quite accomplished. So good, in fact, that she is second in charge. Melvon is head of the guards and enjoys that position.

Everything is almost right in the world.

"You waited," Grim says, surprised, as he walks back in after checking on Brody. "Now, I've been dreaming of how you taste." He tears at his shirt, and it falls to the floor, making me smile.

"Have you?" I whisper, spreading my legs a little wider.

"Yes, and I bet it's like Heaven, just how I remember."

I can't help but laugh as he gets down on his knees in front of me.

The Angel of Death.

On his knees for me.

What a story that could be...

About the Author

USA Today Best Selling Author T.L. Smith loves to write her characters with flaws so beautiful and dark you can't turn away. Her books have been translated into several languages. If you don't catch up with her in her home state of Queensland, Australia you can usually find her travelling the world, either sitting on a beach in Bali or exploring Alcatraz in San Francisco or walking the streets of New York.

Also by T.L Smith

Black (Black #1)

Red (Black #2)

White (Black #3)

Green (Black #4)

Kandiland

Pure Punishment (Standalone)

Antagonize Me (Standalone)

Degrade (Flawed #1)

Twisted (Flawed #2)

Distrust (Smirnov Bratva #1) FREE

Disbelief (Smirnov Bratva #2)

Defiance (Smirnov Bratva #3)

Dismissed (Smirnov Bratva #4)

Lovesick (Standalone)

Lotus (Standalone)

Savage Collision (A Savage Love Duet book 1)

Savage Reckoning (A Savage Love Duet book 2)

Buried in Lies

Distorted Love (Dark Intentions Duet 1)

Sinister Love (Dark Intentions Duet 2)

Cavalier (Crimson Elite #1)

Anguished (Crimson Elite #2)

Conceited (Crimson Elite #3)

Insolent (Crimson Elite #4)

Playette

Love Drunk

Hate Sober

Heartbreak Me (Duet #1)

Heartbreak You (Duet #2)

My Beautiful Poison

My Wicked Heart

My Cruel Lover

Chained Hands

Locked Hearts

Sinful Hands

Shackled Hearts

Reckless Hands

Arranged Hearts

Unlikely Queen

Connect with T.L Smith by tlsmithauthor.com

www.ingramcontent.com/pod-product-compliance
Lightning Source LLC
Chambersburg PA
CBHW070539120726
47909CB00007B/2184